DANNY'S WORLD

(From Handicapped to Hero)

The Story of a Little Boy
Who Changed Society…
FOREVER

John Holt

Published by:

MaxHoltMedia

© 2015 John Holt

Published by MaxHoltMedia
303 Cascabel Place, Mount Juliet, TN 37122
www.maxholtmedia.com

Cover design by: Max Holt Media

Cover Photo – ID 50626525 © George Kroll | Dreamstime.com

ISBN-13: 978-1-944537-00-5

CONTENTS

JOHN HOLT

AUTHOR'S NOTES

In the era of my childhood, it seemed to me, though it was unspoken, that handicapped children were regarded as not quite human enough to be a part of life as 'normal' people did.

There was an unspoken understanding that it was acceptable to keep them out of sight and unmentioned, unless asked. Outside of their own family they simply did not exist. Many were put in asylums and forgotten. Little, if any, effort was made to change this. They were orphans in their own homes and families. There were exceptions, but they were too few to influence any changes.

When my grandson Toby was born with Spina Bifida, this started me on a journey to my past memories of special needs children, as they are now called. Much of what is in this book I owe to Toby. I have done some research, but most of my sources are my memories of people and a time when these little disabled, handicapped, children were shoved into the background of daily life and given enough necessary to keep them alive until they died.

I have never forgotten these things. It is my desire you will not forget them either.

History is my second preference. If I had not been involved in music education, I would have been a historian. I have studied extensively the Civil War and The Second World War. I have referenced the Nazi treatment of children and adults in this book. Their barbaric methods have left the world permanently appalled.

I have used a mix of fact and fiction to tell this story. The facts are there to bring the real story to you, the reader. The fiction is to add the truth of the characters existing then and to some extent still exist today.

My research revealed the harsh, brutal and vicious treatment the handicapped children received in some of the asylums and care homes.

I have not identified any specific religion or church. The church referenced here serves to show the important part the church has played in helping to get these special children out of the grip prejudice and into the sunshine of truth and love.

DEDICATION

First and foremost, I want to dedicate this book to my wife Lon Nell. Above all others, she has been my faithful mate and sweetheart for more than fifty three years. Her insight helps me align my impulsive, creative thoughts in a practical way. She knows me better than all others and she is the ideal wife.

Second, I want to dedicate this book to my grandson Toby. He is the real inspiration for the story. He has had more than thirty surgeries in his nine years of life. He has gone from crisis to crisis without complaining or whining.

He also represents all the little 'Tobys' who have suffered while we were learning. He is one of the reasons much has been accomplished toward getting our special children out of the darkness of fear and superstition into the sunlight of love and acceptance.

Also, this book is dedicated to Carrie Fabian Holt, Toby's mother.

Amid the rapid pace of living in this twenty first century, she is still a mother in the traditional way. She stands by her child and goes the extra mile to learn all the medical things she needed to know when there are no doctors at midnight and an emergency occurs. She has given up many things in order to give the best of her time and love to her children. If there is such a thing as an angel in human form, she is it.

It is not so much that I was inspired to write this book; the truth is, I could not help doing it.

FOREWORD

The story you are about to read is both moving and yet difficult to read because of the prejudices society brought upon children (and their families), who were born with special needs or disabilities, almost a generation ago. It reveals what happens to the human heart when we become so prideful that we view ourselves better than others. It also uncovers how their prejudices were based on superstition, fear, and ignorance about the human body, disabilities, and disease.

On the other hand, it also teaches a very important lesson. That ALL people are people. It's important to remember this when you meet someone who looks, moves, speaks, eats, or lives differently than yourself. They desire to be known as "Toby or Danny," not as that person with Spina Bifida or any other label the medical dictionary has given to their differences. If you know one person with a diagnosis, then you know one *person* with that diagnosis. Each one desires to be known as a person first.

The author is my father-in-law, a person who has shown great love to his grandson. His unending perseverance in teaching a little boy to sing, when he barely had enough breath to speak because of his tracheotomy, endears him to my heart. Toby has taught all of us how to endure through hardship with courage and a wide smile.

I hope you will allow this book to touch your heart and fill you with resolve to treat those with disabilities as people who desire love, kindness, encouragement, and respect just like yourself.

Carrie Holt
Lewis Center, OH
Toby's Mother

Chapter One

FREAK

"Roscoe, I never knew it took so long for a baby to be born". James Smith was a first time father, and Roscoe, his coon dog, was a good listener.

From inside James heard his new born son announcing to the world he had arrived.

Dessie, Dr. Ramsey's nurse came to the screen door. "Mr. Smith, you have a baby boy. Dr. Ramsey said you can see him in 20 minutes, he needs a bath and a check up."

Dessie was a third generation black mid-wife. Her mother knew Dr. Ramsey from past times of working together and she wanted Dessie to get some training from a medical doctor. She was young but already had more than twenty deliveries to her credit.

This was the Smith's first child. They had problems conceiving and they were excited. They had already decided on names if it was a girl or a boy.

"James, you can come in now and meet your son, James Daniel Smith." Dr. Ramsey held the door open.

James looked at the squirming, wiggling, red faced baby and hesitated. It suddenly hit him, "I have a son, who will carry my name for life." His elation was short lived.

"James, sit on the bed next to Loretta, I have to show you something." Dr. Ramsey lifted the blanket from the baby's feet and pointed to a hairy growth on his right foot. "This is nothing to worry about. I have seen things like this before. It is just a surface growth that can be removed with simple surgery in due time."

James's reaction surprised everyone. It was as though he suddenly became a different person. "No! No! No!" His eyes wide in shock. "This is not my son, there are no freaks in my family."

He went to the kitchen, took down a quart jar and slowly drank as he stared at the floor and mumbled quietly over and over, "There are no freaks in my family."

He felt Dr. Ramsey's hand on his shoulder, "James, let me explain this. This happens sometimes, people just don't talk about it much. Do you remember Jack Womack's boy Albert? Do you remember he was born with no left ear. It was just a small button instead of an ear. Remember Ira Luttrell's girl? She was handicapped."

James continued to drink as he stared at the floor. "Dr. Ramsey, I just can't understand how this could happen to me! We have no history of freaks in my family. Somebody else is this deformed boy's father, not me."

"Listen to me James, Dessie has a baby boy who is almost totally deaf. Because he can't hear, he will never talk very well, unless we could get hearing aids."

James just shook his head. "This is not my son and I won't rest until I find out who did this to me." He stepped back out of the kitchen and looked at his wife. "Loretta, you may as well tell me now. You know sooner or later I will find out anyway"

Their Pastor had just arrived. He walked over to console James.

"James, I just heard about your new baby. I have known you since your family moved here nine years ago. I've known Loretta's family twenty or thirty years. I understand how you feel. Nobody thinks bad of you or your family. They sympathize with both of you. Dr. Ramsey said simple surgery could give Danny a regular size foot."

"Pastor Richards, I know there are no freaks in my family."

James continued on his crusade to find Danny's real father. The tendency of small minded people in the community to add gossip and supposition to the situation only inflamed James further. He successfully made a fool of himself.

Loretta loved her little prince. She did her best to shield him from James' verbal beatings. For the most part she succeeded. She sang as she nursed him to sleep gently stroking her hand through his curly blond hair and telling him he would grow up to be a great man. She could not have envisioned just how true that would be.

Danny struggled to crawl at first. Gradually he got used to advancing with his left leg and dragging the heavy right foot. Loretta would call him to her across the room. The encouragement was all he needed. He began to walk later than most babies. He would put his left foot forward and drag the heavy right foot, and then he simply walked as though he had a limp, and then a light step and finally a heavy step.

The right leg soon developed

noticeably larger muscles, but he was walking. The growth did not cover his foot, just a bulge at the ankle, and with the weight, more muscles grew also.

James often lashed out at Loretta, frustrated. "Nobody wants to hire me!"

Loretta was gentle, "James everybody knows about your drinking. You're a good man with machinery, but you are a risk."

Over the years James had seldom kept a regular job. Loretta met him when she worked in her father's office at Martin's Lumber Company. She had dropped out of school her junior year to care for her terminally ill mother, who had cancer and then died within a year. She and James married soon after.

James's health had grown steadily worse with his drinking. Loretta had looked for work but she just managed a few short term jobs, nothing steady but her administrative skills kept her in demand.

James finally got a short term driving job with a lumber company hauling logs out the hills north of town. It paid well and would maybe develop into a regular job.

"Well, look men, here comes the cowboy!" The other drivers were amused with his attempt to look like a cowboy. Nobody knew James cut out the latest pictures of cars, pickups, and cowboy movies and put them on his garage wall. Loretta knew but gave it little attention.

Everyone also knew about Danny's foot. James had begun abusing Loretta when he was drunk, and eventually included Danny also. He would say, "Who do you really call your daddy?" Danny would be terrified. Loretta tried to hide the evidence of abuse.

James was beyond the reach of reason and logic. He chose to live in his dark world of obsession.

JOHN HOLT

Chapter 2

MASTER MECHANIC

James Hobert Herrington was an only child. Hob was only eighteen years old, but he was a brilliant mechanic. He had become one starting at twelve years old and over the years by trial and error, repairing farm machinery that broke down through normal use. He had forgotten how many times he heard his Dad say, "Hob, the old tractor won't start again, can you fix it?" Somehow he always 'fixed it.' That necessity had made him grow up fast.

His Dad had hoped his son would take over the farm but Hob really preferred mechanical work to farming. He was already in demand and the barn had more cars in need of repair than cows or tractors. Some people said he was born with a wrench in his hand.

When Hob's father had died he moved his business into the old Schumann Lumber Company building at

15

the edge of town. They got it for the taxes. The main building was almost fifty yards long and divided in the middle. A two bedroom house and two tool sheds came with it.   He moved in with his mother.

Dr. Ramsey arrived at the shop. "Hob, will you go and look at Loretta's car and see what it would take to get it running. James neglects her and Danny and she really needs a way to get around. She will lose her job without a car. I will pay you whatever it takes." Dr. Ramsey was always one to watch out for people.

Loretta opened the door when Hob knocked. He said, "I'm going to take your car to the shop and get it running for you."

"But Hob, I can't--"

"I know. I have some old parts from other cars that will work on yours, they are free."

He saw a small face peek from behind Loretta. "Hi Danny, my name is Hob. Will you shake my hand?"

A small hand came out from the folds of Loretta's skirt. Loretta explained. "Hob, James treated him so rough he is afraid of men, but he's not afraid of you. I'm surprised."

Hob smiled. "Danny, I have two pieces of candy. I think we should eat candy together, don't you?"

A good friendship started to bloom right then and there.

Later James come to the garage to see about Loretta's car. He was more than drunk this time.

"I hear you made friends with Danny with your candy," he said, "All he talks about is Mr. Hob who fixes cars. Are you sure you don't have more than a casual interest in him?" His stare became a glare at Hob and he turned mean. "So the truth finally comes out who Danny's real father is. I would never have suspected you. I always considered you a gentleman."

"I am a gentleman," Hob said. He then grabbed the collar of James' coat behind his neck and lifted him up so his feet barely touched the floor. He then put him in the tool shed behind the garage to sober up.

As he was about to close the door, James lunged for him. "I'm going to teach you a lesson Mr. James Hobert Herrington. You should be ashamed of this."

Hob usually took pity on James, but this was too much. He buried his big grease covered fist in James's jaw below his right eye and said, "This will be an added part of your hangover later."

"Not bad for a mechanic."

Hob turned to see Sheriff Greer smiling through his car window. "I felt like I ought to stop by when I saw James come in. I thought he might cause some trouble but it looks like you have it under control"

Hob smiled. "No problem here Sheriff, thanks for stopping by." He watched as the Sheriff drove away.

Hob worked for a couple of hours and then checked on James in the shed. He had fallen into a *drunk sleep.* Hob woke him and drug him out to the street. He made sure he could stand on his own. He then told him to go home and sent him on his way.

When he came back in the shop Scooter Johnson was waiting. He had been hanging around nearby until everyone was gone.

He said, "Hob, I need to talk to you private like. We have not met, but I'm told you are the man who can help me. I know you don't drink and I know you are the best mechanic for miles around. I need you to look at my car and tell me what to do."

Hob had heard that Scooter was a

moonshiner and one of the most important tools he needed was a reliable fast car.

Scooter started it and Hob listened to the motor and then turned it off.

"There's nothing wrong with the engine. The Ford flathead is a good motor, but to do what you are doing you just need more power. I can think about it and see what I can do."

After Scooter left Hob turned and saw someone entering the other end of the huge garage. Walking closer he saw that it was the Sheriff who had come back.

As he got closer, the Sheriff said, "Hob, those moonshine boys are too fast for me, can you tune up my car a bit?"

Hob grinned at the irony. "Sheriff, I would need authorization from the county to do anything other than a standard tune up on you car." Hob wished he could tell him what he needed most was to be a better driver.

Chapter 3

DEATH OF THE COWBOY

"Loretta, I've come about James." Sheriff Greer and Pastor Richards never came at the same time with good news. She invited them in and they sat down. After a few moments the Sheriff said, "I'm sorry to have to tell you, James has been in a wreck."

"Is he alright, what happened?!"

"He couldn't stop his truck on the ridge road. He hit the truck in front of him."

"Was he drinking?"

"No, his pants cuff caught under the brake pedal and he could not stop in time. I guess he didn't think to use his left foot on the brake."

She feared to ask, "Is he dead?"

"Yes, he was crushed by the logs on the truck in front of him."

Loretta was stunned and said, "He just had to have those big oversize pants with the big cuffs. He thought it made him look like a cowboy." She was torn between grief for him and relieved there would be no more drunken beatings for her, or for Danny.

Loretta recovered a little from the shock. "Pastor, and you too Sheriff, I want to show you some things I found in the garage."

She led them to the garage and as they looked around she explained.

"James cut out pictures of cars in magazines every year when the new ones came out. He put them on the walls as you can see. He also put any cowboy movie posters he could find. But I found this and it really bothers me. I didn't know they made movies like this."

She pointed to a movie poster about freaks that James had hung up. "See this, this makes me sick to think they would put people like this on display, like weird animals or something."

It was a 1932 MGM movie poster. It was: *TODD BROWNING'S AMAZING*

PRODUCTION OF FREAKS.

She slowly asked, "Could this be what made James afraid to admit Danny was his son?"

The Pastor looked at her, "I don't know, some people seem to be attracted to stuff like this and they can't leave it alone. I can't make sense of it myself. There have been people among us for years, with abnormal things like six toes or crooked legs or so limited that they can't speak or take care of themselves. Some people are suspicious that it means something bad about them. Some just don't say much about it, they just hide children like that and live with it."

After James' death and the funeral no one in town wanted to say it out loud, but Loretta now really had one less problem. She did grieve for James, but she felt her task of helping Danny grow up with his big foot would be much easier.

Still, it would not be simple since people were reluctant to bring their handicapped, or otherwise less than normal children out into society. But she was determined to treat Danny as just a normal boy.

The day after the funeral Loretta answered the phone at home.

It was Hob. "Loretta, your car is ready. I will bring it by in the morning and you can bring me back to the shop."

Loretta said thanks and that tomorrow would be fine.

The next morning she greeted Hob and he stepped inside to wait for Loretta to get Danny ready.

Soon Danny came toward him with his hands out.

Hob smiled, "What does he want?"

Loretta said, "He wants to touch you. James would never allow it. He would yell at him and say, *'Don't touch me you freak.'*"

Hob picked him up and held him face to face close to his chest.

Danny seemed overjoyed as he said, "Daddy, Daddy."

Hob was surprised. "Does he think I'm his father?"

"No, he just used to cry after James and said Daddy over and over."

Danny touched Hob's face and leaned close to his chest. Hob didn't know quite what to say, but he liked making Danny happy.

James had been gone about a year. Hob had thought about Loretta often, but he felt it might seem improper to call on her. He knew she and Danny often had breakfast at Mildred's Diner. Mornings were always crowded there.

Hob was glad when he saw Loretta come in with Danny. He waved her to his table, since there were no other empty places.

Hob had started noticing what a

beautiful girl she was, about five feet four inches tall with blondish brown hair with curls that bounced when she walked. She was petite and seemed to almost walk on her toes.

They enjoyed breakfast together and Hob hoped it was the start of something between them.

Danny had become a good student in school and as he continued to grow so did the growth on his right foot. He was subjected to jokes, derision, and sometimes imitated in schools skits to much laughter and applause.

The school bully, Gerald Jones was Danny's chief antagonist. He would drag his foot and say, "Guess who I am?!"

Danny tried his best to ignore him and the others but it *hurt* every time they teased him.

One day Loretta heard a knock and she smiled when she answered the door. "Hob, what brings you today?"

Hob had grown up without siblings, but he loved children. He had come to see Danny.

"I need Danny's help," he said, "I can't fix this fire truck and this train. I wonder if he could help me." He brought out a toy fire truck with a wheel that needed to be put on, and a toy train that he could not make the coupler connect to the other cars.

Danny almost climbed into the box with the toys. Hob sat on the floor cross legged and gave Danny the fire truck. "Danny, I'm not sure how to put this on. I just can't fix it."

Danny looked intently at the toy truck and turned to Loretta. "Mom, you can go in the kitchen now, us men have work to do."

Loretta's smile broadened. "OK, just call me if you want something to drink."

That day was a turning point for Danny. Hob's visits became more frequent, always to... see Danny, and

Danny came more and more out of his shell. Loretta was starting to allow herself to imagine a new future.

But, all of that, and the entire world changed as church was dismissing on December 7, 1941.

The news came first by radio; Japan had attacked Pearl Harbor an hour earlier and America was plunged into a world war.

Hob was torn between a sense of duty to his country and his concern for his mother. Dr. Ramsey and Pastor Richards were his trusted advisors at times like this, so he sought counsel from them. They told him to follow his heart.

The war soon came closer to home with some of Hob's friends leaving to serve in the Army. He felt he had to do his part too, so he volunteered and was scheduled to leave in two months. He had the extended time to arrange things for his mother.

He arranged for Alvin Luttrell to keep the garage going. He told Loretta Alvin would look after things for her when she needed something done since he was an old family friend.

Hob's biggest dread was the coming *goodbye* he would have to say to Loretta and Danny. He knew Danny wouldn't understand why his new best friend had to go away.

JOHN HOLT

Chapter 4

ARISTOCRAT

Claire Rogers was relatively new in town. She was the second wife of the late Dr. Charles Rogers. The Rogers were some of the first people to settle in the area. His family dated back to the early 1800's.

Charles went to medical school and pioneered several surgical procedures. He came back to his roots about two years before his wife died.

He met Claire at a medical convention in Chicago. He was a widower and lonely, easy prey for someone such as Claire. She was fifteen years younger and seemed to be of some distinct nationality other than the local people.

There were some in the community from other countries, and there was a neighborly feeling among them. Claire seemed to work hard to stay outside of that group, resisting being identified with the local folks.

She was quick to make it known she was wealthy. Dr. Rogers had built a lodge resort on ten acres near the bend of the river five miles from town. He finally gave it to the state for a park with the condition Claire would have lifetime room and board.

The local women disliked Clair's *snooty ways*, as they called them. She refused their invitations to visit with them in gatherings and she avoided them in public. She soon squandered her late husband's respected reputation with her asinine, tyrannical, personality. She seemed to be loathed by almost everyone. And, she had secrets she desperately wanted to keep hidden.

Dr. Ramsey knew how Claire met Dr. Rogers. He was in Chicago with Dr. Rogers; they were friends. He knew Claire's secrets, but she did not know he knew.

Claire acted like royalty among

peasants. She was trying to be something she was not, with her gaudy dress and fake mannerisms. There was a vulgar coarseness about her that was obvious to people.

Maggie Bourland said it like this, "She is more than just an unhappy, frumpy, woman; much more."

Claire made a few exceptions to her exclusive aloof attitude about the local people. She liked Inez Turksen, an elementary school teacher. She also liked Elmer Bunsen, an illiterate mentally limited local man, and Jerome Wiggleman, a man known for his thirst for money. He would do almost anything to make more.

Inez was especially dear to Claire. They shared a common loathing for *what they called* freaks and *different* people. No one saw this in Inez until Claire came to town. Inez was fascinated with ghosts, evil spirits, supernatural things, and often told related stories to her class.

Saturdays were sort of *town days* for a lot of the country people. They came to buy stuff they needed, sell produce and canned vegetables and jams and jellies, and generally catch up on their social life.

On one such Saturday Claire drove by in her new Cadillac convertible.

"I just find it hard to like her," somebody said, watching her drive by, "My wife thinks she is up to something bad, but she can't quite figure it out."

Charlie Breckler did welding and blacksmithing locally. He replied, "I remember something Dr. Ramsey said about her. He said, *'You can't make a silk purse out of a sow's ear.'* Now that didn't make sense until he said it like this, *'you can't make a chicken salad sandwich with chicken feathers.'*

"Now I take that to mean Claire is trying to be somebody important, she just doesn't have anything inside to do it with."

Charlie's friend added. "Old Doc Ramsey is a lot smarter than he lets on. I know he is educated but he also has a lot of good sense. He can see things about people before the rest of us figure them out."

Danny walked into the kitchen to get his school lunch. He saw a hand written recipe on the stove. It read,

HOMEMADE SUGAR PIES

He looked intently into his lunch sack with an obvious question in his eyes.

"They're homemade sugar pies," Loretta said, when she saw the question on his face.

Danny was able to take his lunch to school but Loretta had struggled to keep food on the table at home. James had left her nothing, other than some scars, both physical and mental.

She was left alone to meet daily needs and keep the rent paid. She didn't mention it to Hob; he had problems of his own, getting ready to report to the Army.

However, Danny found to his delight, that his homemade lunch with those delicious fried pies gave him an advantage none of the other kids enjoyed. Loretta had taken biscuit dough, rolled it out flat, cut it in circles, sprinkled sugar and cinnamon on it, folded it into a half circle, and fried it like she did chicken.

It didn't take the kids at school long to learn what a delicious dessert Danny brought every day. It wasn't unusual to hear conversations like:

"Hey Danny, want to trade half a pie for my sandwich?"

"Ok, Bobby, and I will give you the other half for your chocolate chip cookies."

Or, "Danny, I'll give you ten cents for half a pie."

Danny always made out with a good, well balanced lunch each day. It was no mystery why Danny Smith was popular at lunch time.

But, he was still the subject of ridicule and jokes at other times. The accusation of being a *freak* was never far away from conversation among the students, and even some of the faculty too.

Inez Turksen used kids like Danny as fodder for her almost daily discussions about ghosts, freaks, graveyard stories, and hazy, fuzzy shadows on full moon nights being seen in the country cemeteries.

She would close the curtains in her classroom to add to the darkness when she turned out the lights and told ghost stories.

No one seemed to challenge the school's policy of allowing handicapped, and *different* children to be characterized in school skits and plays.

One day Danny asked Loretta, "Mom, why do people think I'm a freak? I don't think I am too different from somebody like Marvin. He has two toes webbed together and nobody says anything about him. And Doris hardly has a thumb on her left hand and nobody thinks she's different."

Loretta put her arm around her precious boy. "Sweetheart, some people have a hard time accepting someone they think of as different. Actually, I think Dr. Ramsey understands things like this perfectly. He is a very wise man. I talked to him about this before you ever started to school. You are too young to understand this now, but you will later."

Across town another conversation was taking place.

"Mom, is Danny Smith a freak?"

The boy's mother knelt in front of him. "What do you mean, a freak, Marvin?"

Reluctantly Marvin said, "He has a big *thing* on his foot and some of the kids call him a freak. Miss Turksen says ghosts don't like people who are freaks, and they go to their house at night and haunt them. But Danny said no ghosts ever come to his house."

"Marvin, do you think I'm a freak?"

"No."

She lifted her right hand. "Do you see this wart on my hand? Does that make me a freak? Your dad has two warts on his elbow, is he a freak?"

Marvin shook his head. "I like Danny. He does not fight with people when they call him a freak. When he was born his dad said he was a freak, but I don't think a big foot makes anyone a freak."

His mother smiled and hugged him. "That's my boy."

School records showed that Danny's grades were among the best, except in Inez Turksen's class. She could not hide her loathing toward Danny. He was a student so she had to teach him in her class. She did not call him a freak in class, but all the students heard her refer to him that way at other times.

Just before Christmas break every year the annual School System Science Fair was held. Danny and his friend Doug Jenson were assigned to work together on their science fair project. They were happy that even their Elementary School classes were allowed to participate that year.

Doug asked, "Danny, how did you discover the can would swell out on the sides when it is hot and would cave in on the sides when it cooled again?"

"Well, I heard jars spew out air when they were opened when they are hot from the sun, but they don't do it when they are cold."

Doug nodded. "Well, you were right. I tried it in my Dad's shop when I found an empty can with a lid on it, and it worked."

Danny was not only very smart but he was a tough little boy, surviving from being the butt of so many jokes. His place of refuge when it all got to be too much was his understanding mother. He knew his friend Hob would understand but he didn't come around much lately. His mom said Mr. Hob was really busy getting ready to fight in the war. Danny didn't understand any of that.

But Loretta would always praise Danny and encourage him to do his best in everything he did. She was even supportive when he started talking about trying out for sports.

"I heard that *freak* Danny wants to play football. Well, he will never play on my football team, that's for sure!"

It was Gerald Jones, Danny's chief

antagonist, spouting off again. Even at his young age, he was thought to be one of the best football players in town. He was definitely the best player in Middle School, just two grades ahead of Danny.

He was good in many positions, but he excelled at quarterback and wide receiver. The Middle School team had a five year losing record, including this year. Many pinned their hopes on young Gerald to change that next season.

He was already being noticed by even the high school football coaches. Gerald was quick to brag about that.

He'd say, "Well, when I get to high school and dazzle those coaches I'll bet I get all kinds of offers to play on college teams." Then he would laugh. "But, little *Danny boy* will get only one offer in high school; from the CIRCUS! They'll want him in their side show of freaks!"

Danny wanted to cry because of Gerald's comments but Loretta told him to be a brave boy and always remember how much he was loved.

JOHN HOLT

Chapter 5

GENERAL PATTON'S HOT ROD JEEP

Hob would be leaving for the Army in a month. He stopped by to let Loretta know. He knocked and the door opened almost immediately, as though he was expected. He could see the skimpy Christmas Tree was still up. Times had been tough and not many people had spent money on Christmas, with the reality of war on the horizon.

Loretta stood in the sunshine in the door in a yellow dress and her *bouncy curls*, as Hob called them. She was a poor girl in simple clothes, but standing there she looked like a princess.

He explained he would be leaving and wanted to tell her the arrangements he had for her car and someone to help if she needed it.

Hob turned to leave when Loretta put her small hand in his huge hand and walked him to the door. She had put a stool beside the door. She hoped this meeting would come and she was prepared. She was five foot four and Hob was six foot six.

She stepped upon the stool and looked him in the face. "Hob, I just can't let you go without telling you I want you to come back to us. This may look too forward but I love you, and I wanted you to know it."

Hob had to catch his breath for a moment. He had physically been hit in the stomach before, but this took his breath away. "Well, I uh, I uh, I love you too. I wanted to say that to you that day in the diner, but I wasn't sure it would sound right at the time." He paused. "I have to leave for the Army, but will you marry me?"

"Yes, yes, yes!" She bounced up and down on her toes with each yes.

Danny had been listening from the hall and did not waste words, "That means you will be my Daddy!"

Danny's life was about to change in

more ways than he imagined.

Loretta was a busy bride to be. She was in a whirlwind of planning, moving, and arranging her new life in the short time until Hob would be leaving. He was working overtime in the shop to get things caught up and setting up things for Alvin. He would keep the business open until Hob came back.

"Hob, how do you like it?" He closed the hood of the car and turned to see Loretta standing in the door to the shop, in her yellow dress.

"I like it!" He smiled.

"I'm moving us into your, uh...our house today. Danny wanted to come to the shop and help you but I made him go to school."

Hob was usually careful to wipe the grease off his hands when he hugged her but this time he forgot. She had brought her stool to the shop. When Hob hugged her without the stool, he long arms reached to the middle of her back, but with the stool she was taller. His grease covered hands pressed black hand prints squarely on her seat. Black hand prints on a yellow dress were easy to see. She didn't care.

Three weeks before he left they married. It was a simple wedding in the church. The place was packed with many good wishes from friends and family. Danny was the ring bearer and he felt like he was king of the world. He wanted to be called Danny Herrington at roll call in school.

The wedding was followed by a home-honeymoon, and a three-week flurry of much packing, crying and reassurances that he would be careful and come home alive.

Finally, Hob and most of the young men in town boarded the train to the Army Training Center in Camp Gordon, Georgia.

The Basic Training was grueling; learning combat skills in the dead of winter. But Hob understood that the Drill Instructors had to be tough to get the men ready to kill the enemy, or to do their best not to be killed.

The toughest part was not seeing Loretta and Danny. Hob got letters from both of them often and he wrote letters home when he could.

After training most of the men were sent straight to the Pacific to fight the Japanese. Having discovered Hob was a born leader of men and a *natural* in everything mechanical, they extended his training to include maintenance of all types of military vehicles and equipment.

The best part was a Merit Promotion from Private straight to Buck Sergeant. That prepared him to be a Maintenance Supervisor in forward combat Maintenance Shops, where he could teach young mechanics the ropes.

After maintenance training and only a two day stop at home Hob was pulled from the Pacific Roster and sent to North Africa, to General Patton's Army forces. Patton was losing a lot of equipment, fighting Rommel's German Panzer divisions and had demanded more mechanics to support his fast moving attacks against the German tanks.

Good mechanics who could keep the machinery of war moving were in constant demand. Patton knew that the Army marches on it stomach, but it needed wheels to get there.

It was August 1942 when Sergeant Herrington, dressed in his Class A uniform, stepped off of the troop ship onto African soil. A ragged looking mechanic with dirty hands and a grease rag hanging from his pocket, was waiting in a jeep to pick him up. He introduced himself as Corporal Joe Stein from New York.

As they drove away the Corporal

looked at Hob's southern mannerisms and his *prim and proper* uniform and shook his head and smiled.

"Hey Sarge, you better change into your *grubbies* on the way. You thought you were goin to HQ to meet the big wigs, but you got a big surprise commin."

Hob didn't understand. "What do you mean? I'm supposed to go to Headquarters to get my field assignment."

The Corporal kept smiling. "Sorry Sarge. They sent verbal orders, with me." He pointed to the back seat. "All that combat gear is yours, including fifty rounds of the ammo; the rest is mine. I am to take you straight to the Division Maintenance Depot, at the front.

"Two days ago Rommel's tanks did a number on a couple of our forward maintenance units; killed a bunch of the mechanics, including the LT."

Hob was sitting there in disbelief. "The Lieutenant was killed?!"

"Yeah. What a shame, he was a great guy, from down south; Alabama, I think. Anyway, they ain't found a replacement for him yet, so it looks like you're going to be the acting Commander til they get another green-horn in."

Hob was shaking his head. "Not me! Are they crazy?! I haven't even been in combat yet."

Joe laughed out loud. "Well, that will be taken care of in about an hour. In the mean time, you'd better start changing."

In the dust and chaos of a shell-pocked road, while dodging every other vehicle known to man, Hob stripped down to his basics and dug his combat uniform out of his duffle bag. He barely got his M1 Rifle checked and the first magazine of ammo loaded before the jeep skidded to a stop at the forward depot.

As they stepped from the jeep Hob

saw a destroyed building across the compound, still smoldering. He put on his helmet and followed Joe into the HQ Tent.

As Hob entered he ran straight into a Major's outstretched hand. He shook it on impulse.

"Welcome, Sarge, I'm Major Jackson, on vacation here from Texas."

Everybody in the tent erupted into laughter. The Major continued. "You must be Herrington. Not a lot of time for formalities. I gotta be out of here in ten minutes."

He pointed to another Sergeant talking on a crank-telephone. "The LT and both NCOs got it in the last German raid. Jonsey there will be your second-in-command for now." Without hardly a breath he led Hob to a grease-pencil chart on the wall. "These are the all the dead vehicles; the ones marked in red are the top priorities. The ones circled in green are General Patton's Staff vehicles...put em on the top of your list."

The aging Major slowly ran his fingers through his scraggly hair. He looked around and found his combat helmet. He put it on and looked at Hob.

"Sorry about this son. War is hell and it looks like the Devil himself is fightin with Rommel." The Major stepped out of the door.

Hob followed. "But, Sir, what about my orders; how am I supposed to go about doing this?"

The Major stopped and then smiled. "Do what the rest of us are doing…just figure it out." With that, he was in his jeep and gone.

For the next six months Hob did what he always did best; he led his mechanics to fix everything that was fixable. He would salvage un-repairable equipment and patch others together.

He survived a frontal tank assault, helping to call in American artillery fire, and two mortar attacks, the last of which left him with a slight shoulder wound. Because of his leadership and bravery under fire he was permanently promoted to Combat Lieutenant.

It didn't take long for his leadership and mechanic skills to get him noticed by General Patton. He led a team out on a priority tank repair mission, that had been called in. When he arrived he discovered General Patton himself waiting beside the his lead tank.

Patton was so impressed with Hob's professionalism that he promoted him to Combat Captain on the spot and reassigned him to command the Maintenance Company at Patton's Headquarters.

Hob had been in North Africa for about a year when the General personally walked into his maintenance office. He was straight to the point.

"Captain Herrington, the Germans are knocking out my tanks faster than I can get new ones, can you set up some more forward area repair shops and put good men and spare parts in them? We need faster repair times."

Hob was the man to get the job done. He could speak the language of anything with a motor in it and he taught his mechanics to do the same.

He discovered that there were very few problems with the new Cadillac V8 engines in the M5 Stuart Tanks. Each one had two engines and some larger trucks ran well with one.

Hob learned the secret of tuning and adjusting those engines so that they produced even more horsepower than designed. He had no idea that later, after the war, his newly-learned skill would be in demand among the local vehicle owners back home, and would also help launch a national sport.

One day he asked permission to put one in General Patton's personal jeep. The General agreed. Hob muffled it down to a quiet hum and the General was proud of his new powerful, faster jeep. He did not ask anything about the details.

Hob and his Maintenance Company followed General Patton around North Africa and Sicily until late 1943. Patton took his maintenance team with him when he was reassigned to England in preparation for D-Day.

Hob ached for home and Loretta and Danny. It sometimes took weeks or months for letters to catch up with the fast moving forces. He would get photos of them from time to time and marvel at how Danny was becoming a *little man*. His little boy would hold up signs for the photos with the words, *"Love you, Daddy!"*

Eventually General Patton took command of the Third Army and lead them onto French soil shortly after D-

Day in June 1944.

Hob had seen more and learned more about human beings than he ever wanted to. Like most G.I.s he hated what the Germans had done to the world but as a mechanic he was fascinated with the Germans' new technologies, especially their jet engine. He wanted to know more about it. It was a new weapon of war, but to him, it was a new engine to discover.

Right after the Third Army defeated the Germans at the Battle of the Bulge Hob participated in liberating a few of the Nazis death camps. He was there when many US airmen were rescued from the Bergen-Belsen concentration camp along with thousands of Jews.

Hob stared in disbelief at the pilots; they were near dead men. His stomach wrenched at the sight of walking skeletons. Their broken, tortured starved bodies were barely alive. He got to meet and talk about it with one of them; Lyle Thompson, a B17 co-pilot from Atlanta. He had been there two years and was near death from starvation and the endless work in barbaric conditions.

He was able to give Hob a perspective on the war that no one else could. He told of horrors, like the routine executions and gassings of Jews and others considered *less than perfect*; in other words, the handicapped and deformed.

"How could one human do this to another human?" he said to those around him.

"I have a son who would have been a victim of this if I lived here instead of in the United States. No one has a right to treat anyone like this just because they have something different about them. Jews don't deserve this kind of treatment just because they are not Nazis Germans, and neither does anyone who is different."

There was a *connection* that formed between Hob and Lyle; they were destined to be friends.

Chapter 6

WORLD RECORD

Three and a half years after Hob said goodbye at the train station, the Germans surrendered. The world would never be the same. After what he had done and seen, Hob would never be the same.

Loretta had tried to maintain some form of normalcy back home; for Danny's sake and her sanity. During those years Danny's big foot gradually grew bigger and the right leg grew stronger.

Dr. Ramsey was involved in the war at home with medical work at the Army Hospital. He checked in on them from time to time, especially to check Danny's foot. He still felt confident the surgery required to remove the growth on his foot would be simple. The size of the leg wouldn't change but the growth would be gone.

While he had been away Hob had written as often as possible. He always made sure to include a separate letter to Danny. He started each of them with; *"My dearest son,"* as Danny's greeting from his new dad. He would tell Danny, "I want you to be brave and look after your mother. She means the world to me and you do too."

Few people would ever forget when the Army Train finally arrived in the fall of 1945. It was loaded with hundreds of local sons and husbands, including Hob. The celebration seemed never ending. Most thought, *"Finally, life can get back to normal."* Hob knew *nothing* would be normal again.

Hob arrived home to a grateful mother, a loving wife and a proud son. Danny was three and a half years older and more mature than Hob could have imagined. Danny could hardly wait to tell Hob that Doc Ramsey thought it was time for his surgery.

Hob told Danny how proud he was of him and that he didn't see any reason to wait. They scheduled the surgery and two weeks later Danny came home from the hospital with just a bandage, where an ugly growth used to be.

Danny's *new foot*, as the children at school called it, was viewed with pride, and not derision. He was no longer fodder for their freak jokes. He was not different than before, they just accepted him without the fear of being called *freak lover*. He just wanted to be normal and to be himself.

Lyle Thompson became good friends with Hob in Germany. He moved to town and became Hob's right hand man. He proved to be a hard worker and learned fast. And, he was honest. He usually ate at Mildred's Diner, since her cooking was better than his. He always sat on the last stool at the end of the counter.

He came for more than breakfast.

He had taken a special interest in the cook. Lyle removed his old worn cap when he came in . He was tall and leaned forward to eat. His thick brown hair often fell over his face without his cap. One morning Mildred overrode her shy disposition and reached across the counter and brushed back his hair. He smiled.

Claire Rogers had never approved of Mildred's cooking, but she ate there several times a week anyway. But today, she was outraged. Mildred could not serve her fast enough. She was seething with anger as she mumbled something unintelligible to herself. When Claire left, Mildred said, "I wonder what she was saying?"

Lyle had watched Claire leave. "She was basically cursing you in German. She called you, and all of us, stupid swine, uneducated peasants, unworthy of good people like her."

"I didn't know you knew German."

"I learned some of the basic language in the prison camp."

Later when Dr. Ramsey came in for coffee Mildred mentioned Clair's tirade to him.

He nodded. "Speaking German? I find that interesting. But I'm not really surprised. I remember her from Chicago. I somehow knew her heavy accent was not British."

"Hey, Danny, Coach wants you."

Danny was sitting on the sidelines with his friends on the *B Team*, watching the football team practice. It was his first year in Middle School and he didn't even try out for the team. He was afraid they would make fun of him.

He didn't know what the Coach wanted so he ran onto the field and reported to him.

"Danny I need a good kicker. Doyle sprained his ankle and we don't have anybody. The game is tomorrow. I have seen you kicking with your friends in the Park so and I want you to try one. All you have to do is keep it straight between the goal posts."

Danny didn't question this opportunity to show what he could do. So, he lined up to do his kick.

Across the street Ed McDonald started the monthly School Board Meeting with the details about the game coming up on Friday. "It sure would good to win one for a change. I don't remember us ever beating North County, and tomorrow is our last game."

Claire was on the Board, serving out her late husband's unexpired term. The second floor windows faced the football field across the street.

When she looked out the window and saw the coach talking to Danny she was outraged. "They are going to let that freak play on our team?! Ed, I demand you put a stop to this immediately!"

"But Claire, there are no rules against boys like him being on the team."

The School Board members moved over by the window to watch. Claire walked away in disgust toward the ladies restroom at the end of a short hallway.

Danny kicked the football. It exploded off his powerful right leg. The second floor was at least one hundred yards from the point of the kick. The ball was perfectly timed to crash through the top window the exact moment Claire was a few feet from the restroom door.

The ball hit her between the shoulders with enough force to send her staggering through the open door. She tripped the flush lever as she struggled to catch her balance. The forward motion dislodged her new wig and it disappeared down the toilet. As if to add insult to injury, the School Board applauded.

Claire stormed out in a rage.

Someone in the room quietly said, "Looks like a World Record to me. Not bad for a freak."

Chapter 7

WHISKEY CARS

It was the next summer, almost two years since the war ended. Georgia, like the rest of the country, was slowing recovering. Businesses were starting to recover and people were making money. One such business was that of providing illegal beverages.

Making moonshine, as they commonly called illegal whiskey, had been a part of the lives of country people for a long time. The demand was always there. For some people who did not drink for pleasure, it was used as medicine.

Prohibition had come and gone, but that had never affected it; there was a real demand for it. To some people, the income it produced was the difference between eating and going hungry.

Since it was a source of income, it was a source of taxes. The problem of enforcing the law fell to local law enforcement most of the time.

But any product, including moonshine, had to be made available to the customer. That transportation need made Hob Herrington a much sought after mechanic.

There was much surplus military equipment after the war. Hob knew most of the men who had the surplus stores and he was always looking for things he could use, since the prices were low. Once in a while he would send Lyle to shops in Atlanta to scavenge for parts.

He came home excited one day. "Loretta, you won't believe what I found. I got this two and half ton truck, 3 used Cadillac V8 engines, a scooter engine, four transmissions and this broken German jet engine all for five hundred dollars. I can make a good tow truck out of the truck. And the other stuff will come in handy. I have men waiting for the engines now."

"Hob, I can see some good in all that except the jet engine. You told me how it works but how can you use it if it's broken?"

"I don't know, but it is the latest thing in airplane engines. The Germans used these at the end of the war. I think it is the engine of the future."

Danny loved working in the shop. He was fascinated with anything mechanical. Lyle was really impressed with Danny's interest and often loaned him some of his tools. Hob mentioned it one day after Danny had gone to school. "Loretta, I really think he has a serious gift."

She nodded. "He seldom asks me for help with something, even if he has never done it before."

Hob took his last sip of coffee and smiled. "There's something else I've noticed."

"What"

"Since he started working with me
he has never mentioned his foot. It's still
larger than the other and he favors it
sometimes but it actually gives him
more strength when he's lifting or
pushing things. I guess it doesn't really
matter to him anymore."

Loretta hugged him. "Well, *DAD*, I
think you have a lot to do with that." She
tiptoed up and kissed him. "And I love
you for it."

As weeks went by Danny started
tinkering with the jet engine. He could
not work on it on the floor. He needed
some place to put it on a work bench
but there was no room on the benches
in the shop.

Hob and Lyle had converted the
Army truck into a wrecker. They built a
flat bed with four by eight oak boards
and mounted a wench on it and then
brought Danny out to see it.

Hob pointed, "Danny, put that jet
engine on the back of the wrecker. All

you need is about two feet of work space. It runs on diesel fuel so you'll have to take a can of diesel and hook the fuel line to it. You may be the first man with a jet powered wrecker truck."

Danny was excited.

Hob had divided the large lumber company building into two equal parts. He did most of his work in the end that opened to the street. The back part was storage and for stuff that would have to wait for parts.

He and Lyle, and even Danny, worked on whiskey cars, as the moonshine cars were called, in the back part. He was not intentionally hiding anything, but the owners preferred to remain anonymous, from the Law. He understood that. They always paid cash when the work was done.

Once in a while Hob would find a pint of clear liquid sitting by his mail box. He did not drink, but to refuse it would be considered an insult. But, it had other uses.

One day Hob brought a box to Danny, who had carved out his own little workspace. He was almost fourteen and was smarter than any of his peers.

"OK, Danny, I'm giving this one to you. This is a three carburetor intake manifold from Edelbrock. Ed Gearhart wants it on his car. Remember we put the engine in it last year? But this time, I won't help you unless you need it. The money is all yours too. I think you are man enough to do the job."

Danny took the car to his corner of the garage. He had he own tools and worked mostly on his own. He had never done this, but he did not hesitate.

When Danny finished the repair Ed was impressed."Well, Hob, I think we have a new mechanic in town." He revived up the engine. "Sounds like it's got the power!"

He praised Danny for his work and

then turned to Hob. "You know Hob, eighty gallons in here is heavy. Can you put more suspension under this?"

"I think so. I've never have done it, but there has to be a way. I'll let you know"

Hob asked Danny to help him on the suspension job. He want to keep teaching him new things. He was going to tell Danny to..."Just sit the extra spring on top of the first spring." But Hob was amazed that Danny had already figured it out.

As Danny worked Hob told him, "It will ride rough except when the extra weight is there."

Danny asked, "How heavy is the extra load?"

Hob thought for a moment, "I think eight hundred pounds."

Ed Gearhart came by to check the progress on his car. He nodded approval of the additional suspension.

He said, "Hob, I don't want to get you tangled up in anything else, but how can I turn off the taillights and brake lights without turning off the headlights."

Danny had heard other whiskey car owners talk about this. He had helped Hob do some work on car electrical systems. He thought about it and he found a way to make it work. He had not said anything, but he tried it on another car and it worked.

Danny replied to Ed's question. He held up a set of switches he had glued together. "I can wire your lights to these two switches and you can flip them on and off when you want to."

Ed smiled in amazement. He took out two twenty dollar bills and laid them on Danny's tool box and walked out.

Hob grinned. His young son was growing into a respected *man* around the shop.

Car racing had become more than

entertainment. They made dirt tracks and had races almost every week. The men who had hot-rod cars always wanted to know who was the fastest and who could handle the tough turns and how different things done to their cars added more power and such things.

J.T. Carpenter was one of the hot-rod owners. One day he stopped by the shop when Danny was there alone. He asked, "Danny will you come to the races after church Sunday?"

Danny's eyes brightened. "I'll ask. It should be ok with my folks. But why, I don't drive that well."

"I like having my master mechanic on hand. I need to know how it corners. I put five hundred pounds in the trunk just to test it."

"Sure, if it's okay with Dad I'll be there."

J.T. put five dollars in Danny's hand. For a boy of his age that made him feel rich.

Most local people saw the hot-rod cars as a passing fad with no real serious future. However, the developments in increasing horsepower with engine modifications, changing gear ratios, and suspensions were not ignored by the automotive industry. Showroom cars would soon benefit from Hob's and others' creative modifications.

Hob's business had become a *one-stop-shop* for anything automotive. He was always one to find more ways to make money for his family. He was even the first one in the area to start renting out cars.

It started when Walter Houseman came by the shop. He employed Dessie's husband, Fred, for years on his farm. Dessie's mother had delivered most of their children.

Walter greeted him. "Hob, do you have any cars you can loan or rent?"

Hob wiped his hands. "I have two, maybe three, why, who needs a car?"

"Dessie needs a reliable car. There is just not much left of that old pickup she is driving. She is a good driver."

Hob pointed. "Well, all I have are these souped-up hot-rod cars. The owners won't be needing them for a few years. She would have to be careful; these cars will run fast if you give them much gas at all. Tell Dessie to come by tomorrow. I'll have something fixed up for her."

"Thanks, I know she will appreciate it."

Maggie Bourland stopped at Mildred's for a quick lunch. She was a tough farm girl, made so by necessity. Her sons had been in the war, and the farm, the sawmill, and the cows were too much for her husband, Shorty.

Mildred leaned over the counter. "Maggie, what brings you to town today?"

"I had to get buy a bearing and a muffler. The truck wheel bearing went out and I ran over a stump and tore off the muffler."

Mildred laughed. "Seems that everybody has problems."

Claire Rogers sat near enough to hear the words *muffler* and *bearing*. She missed having an excuse to get into the social scene so she decided to go see Hob.

"Hob, I think something is wrong with my car, can you look at it?"

"Mrs. Rogers, this is a new car, is something broken already?"

"Well, I don't really know, but I think it may be the muffler bearing."

Hob smiled to himself, *"She doesn't know that a muffler is simply part of the exhaust system. It doesn't have bearings."*

He said to her, "It will be later today, but we'll see what it needs."

Hob's mother had come to the shop

and was listening. "Hob Herrington, you should be ashamed of yourself, taking advantage of that poor woman. You know she knows nothing about cars."

"Mom, I must admit, I am having a hard time being ashamed. I just could not pass this up. Besides, she isn't poor and she thinks she is the smartest person in the whole world."

When Claire came back later that day Hob wanted to have a little more fun. He said, "Well Claire, I'm sorry I have bad news for you. You were right, it is the muffler bearing. This is a special car. I work on very few new Cadillacs, and yours is a convertible. It is so new there are none in the junk yards to get parts from.

"I will have to special order the parts from the factory and I will also have to buy special tools. I will need a left-handed screw driver and a snorkel jointed pipe wrench. Also, on this car, I will have to unplug the electric on the ash tray."

Claire was nodding like she understood. "Don't worry about the cost, I have the money."

Hob could hardly contain his laugh. "The cost will be around fifty dollars if I don't run into any problems."

Claire looked serious. "Let me know when it's fixed and I'll pay the bill." She then turned and left.

Hob finally let out the smile he had been stifling, and turned to finish getting the rental car ready for Dessie.

Danny had been listening from nearby. He walked over. "Dad, you know there's no such thing as a left handed screwdriver and a snorkel-jointed pipe wrench or even an electric ashtray." He paused and then smiled. "Oh...you were just having some fun with her ignorance, right?"

Hob nodded and smiled.

Dessie liked the new fast car. She had to adjust to slowing down on corners and even on gentle curves. Her old truck didn't have nearly this much power. This one spun the wheels each time she let out the clutch in low gear.

She was slowly getting used to it, as noted by the Sheriff. He saw Hob in town and said, "Hob, are you aware you unleased a speed demon on us? I clocked Dessie at seventy five miles per hour at Bailey's farm, just before she missed the curve and drove through his chicken house. And that's the second time. He wants me to arrest her. With all the chickens she has already killed he is going to be eating chicken salad sandwiches, chicken and dumplings, and chicken soup for the next six months, unless she drives through the chicken house again."

Hob laughed. "Give her time Sheriff, she'll get the hang of it."

When Hob got back to the shop Dessie was waiting for him with the hood of the car raised. She was wiping the sweat of concern off her face. "Mr. Hob, I think maybe I done something to this car. It's got a funny noise in the motor."

Hob looked around the engine and then burst out laughing. "Lyle, Danny! Look at this,... ever see anything like this in a car?"

They both came over and after a few seconds, joined in Hob's laughter. Lyle finally said, "No, no, that's the first time I ever saw anything like that."

Dessie was confused. "Is it broke or something?"

Hob strained to control his laughing. Lyle and Danny still roared with laughter.

"No, Dessie, it isn't broke, it's alive! It's a live chicken, stuck behind the engine!."

Dessie looked and then joined in the hilarious moment.

Chapter 8

OUT OF DARKNESS

Danny never missed a chance to inspect new cars. When Henry Bennet stepped out of his new Buick and walked into the shop, Danny looked it over. As he looked in the window he saw a small girl looking back at him.

He smiled at her. "Hi, how are you today?"

The unexpected attention brought an excited response. She sat up as tall as she could on the pillows under her arms. He could tell she was a special child.

Henry noticed Danny's interest in his daughter. He went over to Hob. "OK if I invite Danny to supper? I heard he is good with children like her."

Hob nodded his agreement. "He's no doctor or anything like that. I think what he has been through gave him a sort of insight about it."

Henry thanked Hob and approached Danny. "Danny, her name is Dolly. Why don't you come to supper with us tomorrow, say 5 o'clock?"

Danny smiled and said, "Yes sir, I'll be there."

That night Danny was talking to Loretta. "Mom, I wonder why he invited me to supper."

She put her arm around him. "The Bennets have been to a lot of doctors with Dolly, and they have all given up. Maybe you can help her. Who knows what could happen."

The next day Danny quit work early. He cleaned up as best he could and changed out of his greasy clothes. He knocked on the Bennet's door at exactly five o'clock. Supper was ready and he enjoyed the family atmosphere, eating, talking and laughing. Dolly smiled a lot but she never talked.

After supper Danny carried Dolly to

a rocking chair on the front porch. Her
mother gave him an apron to hold her
upright and showed him how to put it
across her chest, under her arms and
through the back of the chair.

Danny asked. "Can she talk?"

Danny saw some moisture in her
eyes. "She tries sometimes when she is
hungry or wet, but it's not really
words."

Danny looked up at her. "Has
anyone tried to teach her?"

"Not really, we don't know if she
can understand us. We know she can
hear but she just doesn't seem to know
how to form the words."

With that, Danny moved a stool
close to Dolly and sat close to her face.
Years earlier his mother had read
everything she could find about
handicapped children. Recently he had
read some of it and found a long article
about teaching such children to talk.
Danny had read it from end to end,
several times. He decided that now

would be a good time to try some of the principles it recommended.

He smiled at Dolly. "My name is Danny." He took her little hand and held it against his throat. "Dan-nee, Dan-nee," He repeated it slowly and distinctly.

Dolly's brow wrinkled as she made an effort to imitate him. He repeated it again still holding her hand against his throat.

She sat up straight, drew a deep breath. Her mouth moved slowly, she pushed her hand against his throat tighter. "Dah-ee, Dah-ee."

"Good, now what is your name?" He kept her hand against his throat and pressed her other hand against her throat. "Daw-wee, Daw-wee", she blurted, "Daw-wee, Daw-wee, me nim Daw-wee."

Danny smiled from ear to ear. He turned to Dolly's mother. Her dad had come out on the porch and watched his daughter saying her first words. They were both hugging each other in tears. They then knelt by the rocker and wrapped their arms around their precious girl, mixing their smiles and tears with hers.

Danny celebrated with them and then did a couple of more demonstrations of Dolly's new-found verbal skills. He then gave her a little hug and whispered, *"I know how you feel."*

As Danny got up to leave the Bennets both hugged and thanked him for the amazing contribution he had made to Dolly's future. He told then how it had helped him to make a difference for someone going through what he had endured. Walking home he knew this would not be his last visit with Dolly.

That night before bed Danny talked to Loretta. "Mom, I wonder how many more there are like Dolly."

She thought, "I know there are quite a few. People have usually just kept quiet about it. That is how is has always been around here."

Danny smiled. "Maybe I can help change that."

Henry Bennet could not stop telling people what Danny had done with Dolly. Parents began to contact Danny to help them with their special children.

Hob was so proud of Danny. "You're becoming a local hero," he said.

Danny blushed a little. "I just know a lot of how they feel and that makes them trust me. They know I'm not a doctor, they just know what I've been through, and they know I understand. And because of you and Mom, I understand a lot of how the parents feel."

More and more people heard about Danny's work with Dolly. Someone suggested a school be started, or some kind of organized way for special children to get help or training. There were asylums, and institutions of various kinds around, but nobody had anything good to say about them. They would rather keep their children at home and do the best they could.

People with the *different* children had been subjected to shame, embarrassment, and superstition. But more and more, with the increased sensitivity to the need that Danny had started, they brought their special needs children out in public. There was a sense of relief among people.

But not to one of the more *notable* citizens.

JOHN HOLT

Chapter 9

BENEVOLENCE?

Hob and Lyle had just opened the shop when the Cadillac pulled up.

Claire rolled down the window. "Hob, I rented the old Benson house. Can you look at the plumbing and the electric? I don't want any problems. Also, can you get me some kind of standby generator? The power goes off in the winter sometimes."

After she left Hob wondered what Claire wanted with a house that big. She was comfortable where she lived and she liked being in town. He had a bad feeling about this.

While Hob inspected the electric and plumbing at the old Benson house two women and a man arrived; people who were not local. They spoke bits and pieces of another language when they thought no one heard them. Hob's uneasy feeling grew stronger.

93

Loretta also had an uneasy feeling lately because of something in the shop office. She kept the books for Hob and managed the office. No one else ever bothered the files; that was until lately.

She asked Hob about it. "Hob, were you in the files yesterday, looking for something?"

"No, why?"

"Some of the files were on the desk yesterday morning. I never leave stuff out like that."

"Hum, that is strange. I'll ask Lyle and Danny."

She shook her head. "Already did, they did not do it."

"The only other person in the shop yesterday was Elmer."

Elmer was a local boy, everyone knew he was slow and illiterate. But he would never do something like that, unless someone told him to. Hob had asked him to do clean up and he paid him for it. Hob was sometimes generous to a fault.

Loretta had an eerie feeling about this. She had a sense of impending danger, but nothing definite enough to act on. She thought maybe Danny might be in danger.

A week later Loretta answered a knock at the door and was greeted by a short middle aged woman. Her gray hair was put up in a bun on her head.

She smiled. "Mrs. Herrington?"

"Yes."

"I'm Elsie Clatterback. We're from the new home for retarded children."

Loretta stopped her and called Hob. He stepped into the hall and came to the door. "I just found out what Claire is doing out at the Benson place. She started what she is calling a home for retarded children."

Hob looked the woman over and said, "These children aren't retarded; they just have special needs."

She just stared at him as he continued. "So, what do you want from us? Is something broken?"

"No," the woman said, "I'm here to tell you it's opening. We already have four children and Danny is the last one on our list. If you will get his clothes and things together, we will be on our way."

Hob stepped between Elsie and Loretta, "Who else is on your list?"

"We have Dolly, Bobby, Sarah, and Susan. Danny will make five. We hope to have more as we find them."

A shock went through Loretta. "There are many children like this, how did you choose these?"

The woman hesitated. Before she could answer, Loretta realized. *"Elmer!"* she whispered to herself. "He's the one that went through our files. Personal information on almost everybody in town is in those files. He's worked for Claire sometime and she has paid him very well. Elmer forms an allegiance to anyone who makes him feel important. He is so naïve and gullible."

Hob picked up the thought. "I'll bet

he heard Danny talk about the children but Danny wouldn't have mentioned last names or addresses."

Loretta looked at her. "How did you get the parents to give you their children since you are a stranger to them?"

She just stared for a moment. "Ah...we told them Danny would be there."

Hob looked at her for a moment and then closed the door in her face. She left without Danny.

The next morning Henry Bennet was waiting when Hob opened the shop. "Hob, I went to the home to visit Dolly and they refused to let me in. Other parents have come to me about this too. They said it would interrupt the children's training program to have visitors until they got them settled in."

Hob said, "They tried to get us to release Danny to them yesterday. I'll make a trip out there and check it out."

He got his tools together and left Lyle to get the repairs started. He headed out of town to make an unscheduled visit to the home. When the same lady came to the door Hob said, "I'm here to do a maintenance check. I have to be sure everything is running and the standby generator motor will start. It will take about ten minutes."

She let him in and he walked down the hallway to the basement door. He heard all the doors shutting just before he walked in. The silence was suspiciously *loud*. He could hear muffled voices; even Dolly's weak little voice. He noted to himself that it was the third room on the north side of the building.

When he left the home Hob went straight to the Sheriff's Office. "Sheriff, something bad is going on out there at the Benson place. Whatever they are doing with those handicapped children, it's not good, I know for sure. I don't want to break the law, so, what can I do?"

The Sheriff made a couple of notes. "I wondered what they were up to. But, I know the parents of these children would not give them their children unless they trusted them. It sounded good to have free room and board and free schooling. I know the people, they are too poor to afford something like this, except maybe the Bennets."

Hob shook his head. "That Clatterback woman said the other parents agreed because they were told that Danny would be there as a student. Otherwise, some of them would have said no."

The Sheriff agreed to do an investigation.

Hob never rushed into anything if he was uncertain about it. Dr. Ramsey was among his most trusted counselors so he asked his advice.

"Hob, I felt from the start this whole thing had a strange flavor to it. People will always respond to kindness, especially if they are poor and it involves their children. And right now everybody is struggling with just making a living.

"I have kept up with how Hitler came to power in Germany since I first heard of him. He was a master manipulator. He appealed to some of mankind's basic weaknesses. He offered something for nothing and no moral responsibility. No one in his right mind would make the promises he did. But desperate people are easily persuaded to follow the food."

Hob was getting angrier by the minute. "Are you saying Claire did something like that to us?"

"I'm not sure I would put her in the same class with Hitler, but her methods are similar."

Chapter 10

KIDNAPPED!

Hob came to the kitchen for breakfast. Danny had just left and Loretta was watching him out the window.

"You need to go talk to Danny. I can tell he is thinking of doing something to get those kids out of that home. I don't want him to get hurt or to hurt anyone else." She understood her son.

Hob skipped breakfast and hurried to catch up with Danny halfway to the shop.

"Dan" was what Hob sometimes called him to express affection, now that he was older. "You're planning to go get your kids?"

"Yes sir." Danny kept walking.

Hob said, "I understand but let me show you how to do it. I've set up some things already. I knew this was coming. You don't have your license yet but go ahead and take the Ford coupe. It has the trunk space you will need. Take the Army blankets from the shop, the clean ones. If anyone stops you just say we were late getting the car done and you were the only one available to test it."

"But, what about----?"

Hob interrupted."Now listen, you need to wait until an hour after dark. The old logging road is a good place to park. Go to the third window on the north side. That is Dolly's room. The window is unlocked. Tell her to get the other children into her room.

"I left the outside basement door unlocked. The power box is just inside on the right. Turn the power off and on several times, and then finally off. The women will all come to check on it, they are afraid of the dark and they'll stay close together. You will need this flash light.

"When they close the upstairs basement door I set it to lock them in. They will never figure out how to open it. Step outside when they open the door. Lock the outside door with the bar I left beside it. They cannot stop you when you take the kids.

"Put the children in the trunk, cover them with the blankets to keep them warm."

"The Sheriff knows this a moonshine car and if he sees it, he will stop you. You will need to think of something if he does.

"Take the children to Dessie. She'll be expecting you. All the children know her and they won't be afraid."

Danny stopped and looked up at Hob, and then hugged him. "Thanks, Dad."

Danny worked the plan perfectly. The children were happy to be kidnapped. He told them to stay quiet, no matter what happened.

The crowd locked in the basement wouldn't know the children were missing until morning, when they finally figured how to get out of the basement.

Danny was not surprised when headlights came up close behind him, followed by flashing lights. He stopped.

The Sheriff walked up to the window. "Danny, I didn't think you hauled moonshine."

"Hi Sheriff. I'm taking Ed MacNamara's pups home to keep while he is gone. He went to the Coon Hunting Nationals again this year. He asked us to take care of them. It's too far to come out here every day."

The Sheriff started walking toward the trunk. "I'd like to see those champion dogs."

Danny quickly walked past him to the back of the car and whispered, "Make noises like you are puppies."

He then looked up. "Sheriff, they are just four weeks old. They're whining. I need to get them home out of the cold. These dogs are important to Ed."

Sheriff offered a knowing smile and

agreed, warning Danny that unlicensed drivers had better stay off the main road. Finally he drove off.

Danny said to himself, *"Whew, that was close."*

Claire Rogers was livid. "Sheriff! Someone broke into the children's home last night and took the children. They beat up Elsie and her help and locked them in the basement. You have to get those children back immediately before--."

"Before what?"

"Before somebody harms them! They have been entrusted to our care"

By now the Sheriff had put two and two together. "Well now, Miss Claire, just hold your horses. I'll check into it but these things take time."

Late the next morning Hob contacted Sheriff Greer. He took Dr. Ramsey, the Sheriff, two city council members and Danny to see the children.

They were having breakfast at Dessie's house. Dolly, Bobby, Sarah, and Susan all shouted at once, "Danny!" They gathered around their hero.

Dessie was used to big crowds around her table. "What we have isn't much, but you're welcome to eat with us."

They all sat down at the big kitchen table. Dessie poured hot coffee. A couple of them buttered a biscuit and they sat there in silence a few moments.

"I have never seen children hurt like this. I don't know if they can tell you, but I can tell by what I see, these people don't love children." Dessie had seen children abused but this was too much.

The Sheriff said, "If you don't mind, keep the children here for a few more days. I will contact Judge Richards. This is too much for a simple solution."

Chapter 11

CONTEMPT OF COURT-CHURCH

The Sheriff's investigation had resulted in Judge William Richards agreeing to hear the case.

On court day the judge entered the court room. Clair, Elsie, Marlene Miller, and Gus Von Bruner were there with their Defense Attorney. Sheriff had also included Inez Turkson to the list of defendants. She taught fifth grade at the school and everyone knew she used her position to promote Claire's ideas.

The courtroom was packed to the walls all the way out to the street. The atmosphere was already thick with rage at Claire's obvious plan.

The judge pounded his gavel and called the proceeding to order. He said, "This is not a trial. We are here to gather information and to hear from those involved in this case. I have no doubt these children are afraid and I want to keep everything calm. I want them to be able to speak without fear of what will happen to them."

He motioned and Dessie brought the children in. As the kids were seated she said, "Your honor, judge, the children told me they were threatened with punishment if they told anyone what was done to them. I'm not sure they will talk about it here."

Judge Richards understood. He stood up, took off his robe and his tie. "Is that better?"

Dessie nodded.

Pastor Richards stood up next. "Your honor, if I may make a suggestion. The church is larger than this room. If you move over there, the children might not be so afraid."

The judge agreed and pounded the gavel. "Court will reconvene in one hour in the church."

An hour later court was called to order in the church. The judge entered.

"I will do without my robe and tie. Lyle Thompson loaned me his coat. I think that will help the children."

"What I have heard around town helps me understand the outrage of you people. I think we can best understand this if the children simply speak for themselves."

The judge moved down to the floor and sat in a chair a few feet from the children on the front pew.

Dolly was first. Her new voice was getting better all the time. "Can Danny come sit with me?"

The judge motioned for Danny to sit by Dolly. She held his hand. The judge told her to say anything she wanted to say. She held onto Danny and said, "I don't feed myself very good. Danny was helping me learn. Miss Elsie say I waste food. She feed me too fast and I choke and spit out the food. She slap me and take away my food. Danny said I do good when I eat slow."

The judge let her pause for a

moment. Then he said, "What else?"

"Mr. Gus get under the cover with me. He said I was who-ree and I have to pay rent. He said if I tell he will beat me. He said nobody will come and get me."

The judge stopped her. "What is who-ree Dolly?"

"Your honor!" Lyle Thompson stood to speak. "I was a B17 co-pilot in Germany. I was two years at Bergen-Belsen concentration camp. I think she is trying to say *hure*. That is what the Nazis soldiers said when they raped Jewish girls. It means a whore."

When Lyle sat down Dolly continued speaking. She held the court spell bound with what she said next.

"Will you make Mr. Gus go away and not hurt me anymore?"

The judge was more than angry. He calmed and said, "Yes, Dolly, Gus will not hurt you anymore."

"Do you pom-miss?"

"Yes, I promise."

"Do you pom-miss like Danny?

Judge Richards had to swallow the lump in his throat. "Yes, I pom-miss like Danny."

"OK."

From somewhere in the room a voice quietly said, "I pom-miss too."

Dolly was best able to speak among the children. "They take away Billy's crutches and make him crawl on the floor. They say he is lazy and stupid. They say he don't pay attention. They put wires on his thumbs and turn on the light. It makes him scream and kick and wet his pants. They clap their hands and say *ton-zin*."

Lyle spoke from his chair. "Your Honor, I think they are saying tanzen. It means dancing. The Nazis tortured us like that."

Dolly continued. "Sarah can't talk much. She can't put her clothes on by herself. She shakes sometime, it's called seizures. When she wets the bed they beat her. They tie the wet sheet around her neck and make her stand outside.

"Susan's eyes don't look straight. They say she is crazy because she wants to eat with her left hand. Miss Elsie say crazy people eat with left hand. They hit her hand to make her stop."

Claire's audacity was still out of control. She couldn't contain herself.

"Your honor, these wild stories are not true. It's natural for children to make up stories to avoid discipline and training. She is lying."

The judge pounded his gavel. "Claire, one more outburst and I will hold you in contempt of court!"

She smirked, "Judge, this is not court, it's a church, remember?"

"Alright Claire, if you insist, you are in contempt of church. All of you can relax in the jail." He had the Bailiff take the defendants out and he recessed for lunch.

After a lunch recess, the hearing

resumed.

The judge spoke. "I have two girls and a boy myself. I am a parent and I'm not sure I can keep my perspective. I have never heard of anything like this."

"Your honor, my I say something?"

Henry Bennet was standing. The judge nodded.

"Dolly is my daughter. She had no real life until Danny came. Then, she was really starting to grow and develop her personality. She was just now able to dress herself and--,"His words chocked in his throat. He sat down.

Judge Richards was ready to address the court but Sheriff Greer was late. The Bailiff brought all the defendants back, except one. Finally he came running in.

"Your Honor, we can't bring Gus in, it seems he has escaped."

Claire screamed in panic, "What have you done to Gussie?"

The Sheriff ignored her. "Your

honor, his name is Gustavus Von Bruner. He is the brother of Eva Vonn Bruner. We all know her as," he paused, "Claire Rogers."

The Sheriff continued. "I can show you the telegram my cousin sent from the Chicago Police Department. Gus is on parole."

There was a deathly silence in the room.

The Sheriff finished with, "The other defendants are old friends of Claire's."

The outrage growing in the court audience told the judge he had better let things cool down. He recessed the court for an hour.

When they reconvened he said, "Sheriff, bring these three here and Inez Turksen too. She had a part in this."

He looked at them for a moment. "I have no legal precedent for reference. This is beyond the pale of moral outrage, it is barbaric. The subject is not just about abusive treatment of handicapped children, it is beyond that. Children like this have been part of human history from the beginning. The ancient Greeks and Romans felt deformed children were born because the gods had been angered. And Nazi Germany had sterilization laws to prevent undesirable people from propagation."

The rest of the summation was addressed to Claire and her friends.

"You hid your true intentions from the parents. I do not believe any of you are parents. You made us think you meant well for the children, but you used our desire to better them to your advantage."

He looked at Claire. "You used the wealth and good name of your late husband to mislead and manipulate. Your sadistic torture was in no way educational. I am convinced you hate anyone who is less than perfect.

"Your kind will always be among us, but we have no desire to be like you. If anyone is truly feebleminded it is people like you. You see no one but yourself. I knew Charles Rogers well; we shared a dorm room at the university. He studied medicine and I studied law. He would be horrified if he knew what you are doing in his name.

"We will not allow you to drag us into the gutter to be like you. We cannot undo what you have done, but we will not allow it to happen again"

Judge Richards paused for a long minute as he struggled to keep his composure. Finally he looked at Dolly and said, "I pom-miss.

He composed himself and made the pronouncement. "The defendants are hereby remanded to appear before the Georgia State Superior Court in Atlanta on a date to be determined. In the mean time they will be transferred to State Custody and held in the County Jail there until such trial can proceed." He looked at Claire and her ladies, and smiled. "Ladies, enjoy their Georgia hospitality. Court adjourned!"

Quietly Claire asked, "But what about Gus?"

Nobody answered her.

A week later Elmer sat with several men around the pot bellied stove in the shop. On cold mornings men would gather there for a while.

Elmer was angry. "Claire lied to me. I would never have helped her hurt those kids. I had no idea this would happen."

One of them said, "I thought you liked her?"

Elmer was still angry. "Dolly is my sister's little girl!"

Lyle changed the subject. "Well, what do y'all think happened to Gus?"

Elmer stood up, put the stick he had been whittling on into the stove and closed the door. He tapped the blade of his knife in his open left hand. "I can just tell you this, he won't be a-hurtin little girls anymore."

Lyle looked up. "Did you do something to him?"

Elmer shook his head. "I ain't sayin, but he won't be a-hurtin little girls anymore."

Elmer headed out but stopped at the door, "Decent men don't hurt little girls."

Gus's disappearance fueled many rumors. Some thought he was hiding in an asylum under a different name. Some thought he'd been seen in Chicago. The rumors even included an unclaimed freight box at the railroad depot in Higgins, Texas. But, nobody knew, for sure.

Chapter 12

FREAKS IN TOWN

There was a sense of celebration on the town square. The next Saturday was what the locals called *town day*. The folks in the county gathered on the square to sell produce, canned fruits and vegetables. Some traded guns and sometimes farm equipment. But mostly they came to catch up on their social life.

But this Saturday seemed different. Twice as many came. The square was lined with pickups, cars, trucks almost in a complete circle.

And this was the difference: at least half of the pickups and cars had special little children proudly sitting on the tail gates, and some on quilts on the grass. There was a breath of freedom about it.

Different children were no longer an embarrassment. Some seemed proud of their *special child*. The powerful taboo was broken.

Danny noticed one family he had never seen before today. They had come in a wagon with a team of mules. They were Tom and Ethel Allman. Danny saw a little smiling boy propped up between two huge water melons.

Danny smiled. "Hi, what's your name?"

Ethel answered for him. "Hez named Billy. We ain't never brung him before, but we heard it was ok to brang him."

Danny pointed and asked. "How did he get the cut on his head? Did he fall or something?"

"No sir, the ghosts done that. They throwed a big rock through the winder when they comed last time. It hit Billy on the head. He cried a lot but he is ok now."

Danny leaned over into the wagon. "Well, Mr. Billy, it's time us men had a talk." He look at Ethel. "May I pick him up?"

She nodded and Danny picked up

the smiling boy. Billy squinted in the sun.

His daddy, Tom, explained. "He ain't been out in the sun before. The ghosts said bad things would happen if we brung him out in the sun. We don't take him outside less it's dark. But we heared about you so we brung him today."

As Danny held little Billy he thought, *"Well, at least this is a start."*

Danny felt sorry for the children and families who had been taken in by the ghost stories of Inez Turksen. After the trial the judge had let her off with a warning but she had been fired as a teacher, because of her cooperation with Claire Rogers.

Danny cuddled Billy close to his chest and felt him snuggling to get closer. Danny looked at Ethel and said, "Ghosts? Do you have ghosts that visit you?"

Ethel nodded. "Yes, they mostly come Saturday night. They tear up our garden and our syrup mill sometimes too. They scratch on the side of the house and we hear big voices."

Danny just smiled and took Billy for a walk. He walked around the square and introduced Billy to everyone. He put his cap on him to shield his eyes from the sun.

When he got back to the wagon he said to Tom, "You say ghosts told you to keep Billy inside unless it was dark?"

Tom nodded. "Yes. They said bad things would happen, they throwed the rock and hurt Billy. That's why hez got the bad cut on the face and the swelled up lip."

Danny could not help but notice Ethel's dress was made from flour sacks and her shoes were old worn out men's shoes. Tom's overalls had more patches than pants showing. They were illiterate and very poor.

He thought, *"Someone is using these people's fear and superstition to do this. I will have to meet these ghosts myself. But who are they? How can I find out who they are?"*

JOHN HOLT

Chapter 13

DON'T HURT BABY BEAR

Hob walked from the Mail Box straight to the middle of the shop, holding up an open letter. "Men, I can't turn this down. This is a letter from State Representative Joe Rudder. He bought the old Taylor farm. I can have everything in the barn, the garage, and the tool shed, just for cleaning them out. There are three cars, a pickup, and a tractor. I can use them for parts."

Hob coordinated a date with Representative Rudder and proceeded to the farm. Lyle brought his pickup, Danny drove the wrecker, and Hob was in his pickup.

When they arrived, as Danny walked around the house to the barn, he saw a little boy smiling and waving from an open window.

"Hi, I'm Danny, what's your name?"

The boy's mother, Barbara, came to

the window.

Danny smiled at her. "I'm Danny Herrington, I'm here with my dad to clean out the barn and garage. Can he talk?"

"He's kind of slow. He can only mumble. There are no understandable words."

"What's his name?"

"His name is Joe, after his father. We call him Joey."

Barbara walked out onto the porch with Joey.

Danny shook her hand. "Well, thank you for all this stuff. We can use it."

Before Danny turned to leave she asked, "Are you the Danny who taught Dolly Bennet to talk?"

Danny paused, embarrassed, "Well, I uh, I uh sort of helped her I guess."

"Well, Danny, we want to invite you and your family to dinner. Joe will be glad to meet you."

"Okay, my dad is in the barn. I'll ask him but I'm sure it will be fine with him and Mom."

Hob and Loretta were excited to get to come to dinner at a State Representative's house. The agreed date arrived and they made the drive to the country.

After dinner everyone sat on the porch and listened to the quiet sounds of the evening.

Barbara talked about their situation. "We moved here to have privacy for Joey, but now I wish we had moved closer to town. Maybe Danny could help Joey too."

Danny was over on the porch swing with Joey, already at work. With Joey's hand on his throat to feel his voice, he said,

"My name is Dann-nee, Dann-nee."

Joey blurted "Dah-ne, Dah-ne."

Danny put one of Joey's hands on his throat and his other little hand on his own throat,

"Your name is Joooo eeeee, Joooo eeeee.

He blurted a full voiced Joyeeeee, Joyeeeee!"

The tears of joy were flowing all over the porch.

Joe Rudder almost shouted "Where did you get this amazing boy?"

Hob smiled and held Loretta's hand, "Well, this lady here raised him."

Loretta smiled and said, "Barbara, you should bring Joey to Town Day."

"What is Town Day?"

She explained the Saturday farmers market, sale day, fellowship. It is special now because many people with children like Joey bring their children. It helps them to talk to each other about the problems of raising a handicapped, different child."

In spite of all the acceptance and openness about special children, not everyone was celebrating.

Claire's influence was not dead.

Some were determined to keep the *different* children in the shadows. It seemed to them that the new freedom to bring different children into regular society was a threat to their way of life. It was not just ignorant people. Some of the efforts to stop this *polluting of society* as it was referred to, came from leaders.

J. Alexander Marlanza was an Italian business leader who had moved to town after the war. He was rich enough to have some influence. He resented the public display of *freaks* on Town Day.

Danny's father, James, had been killed in the truck accident years ago. Since then, his cousin Ernest Smith, was intent on keeping the family prejudice alive, demeaning handicapped or disabled people every chance he got.

Often in public he would reference his new Italian friend and say, "It's not just us Americans. A lot of people don't like it. They just don't say so in public."

Ernest's drinking buddy, Leonard

Cox drank the same poison of prejudice, publically at every opportunity.

One day Ernest and Leonard saw the Sheriff out in front of his office. They approached him and Ernest said, "Sheriff, we don't want to cause you any trouble, but we are going to stop these Saturday circuses on the town square. Enough is enough. We won't do anything his week. We want to give you time to talk some sense to these people."

The Sheriff smiled. "Boys, you better not cause any trouble or you'll be pressing the sheets in one of my beds in the jail." The two just turned and left.

The Sheriff was concerned that they might not take his advice so he asked that a Town Council meeting be called to solve this problem. No one wanted to oppose the influential people or some of their own neighbors, but these children were citizens too.

Finally Dr. Ramsey spoke up. "This week is decision week. These trouble makers have drawn the line in the sand. If we let prejudice and fear and ignorance rule in this, we may as well go back to living in caves and wearing animal skins. We cannot modify the truth to accommodate ignorance and prejudice.

"Even though these are our relatives and neighbors, they are acting like any other tyrant. They only respond to force stronger than their own. If they insist, I will dust off my old twelve gage shotgun. I have never shot anyone in my life. I have patched up some who were and it is nasty what a shotgun can do. But we have sacrificed too much to let these ignorant tyrants destroy it."

"You can count me in too. I have seen too much good done for my girl Dolly. I will not let her new life and freedom be stolen, even by my neighbors." Henry Bennet meant business and it showed. He paused and then said, "I have a double barreled twelve gage too. One barrel for ignorance and one for tyrants."

The Sheriff and the Council members worked on a plan to stop any violence from the prejudiced ignorants who were threatening the Town Day activities a week and a half later.

Early that Saturday morning the group of prejudiced misfits the Sheriff had warned were gathered on Ernest's front porch, about a mile outside town, loading their rifles and shotguns.

He stepped off the porch and said, "OK, boys, get ready to scatter these freaks like chickens. We have to be tough to show them we mean business."

There were nine men in two pickups. They envisioned themselves saving their town and preserving their way of life.

Sheriff Greer was waiting at the

edge of town, his patrol car blocking the road. He and a couple of citizen deputies were standing in the road.

The pickups stopped and Ernest got out.

The Sheriff spoke loud enough for all to hear. "Men! I'm not here to stop you with force. I came to tell you that you will face at least thirty shotguns and rifles if you do this. You can go home or you can go into town peacefully, or you can go ahead and get yourselves shot. You know what they say: IF YOU HURT BABY BEAR, MAMA BEAR WILL GET YOU. And mama bear is waiting for you in town."

As the Sheriff stood there the misfits gathered for a close discussion. Ernest was mad and still wanted to charge into town, to rid it of the *freaks*. But cooler heads prevailed and outvoted Ernest. Finally he turned to the Sheriff.

"Okay, Sheriff, you win, this time. But when the whole town is polluted with those little *freaks* it will be your

133

fault!"

The pickups turned around and left.

The whole town was buzzing about the confrontation with...*IGNORANCE.*

Town Day was quiet, peaceful and successful. More and more families with disabled children smelled the fresh air of acceptance.

During a gathering of friends at Hob's house Loretta was discussing those ignorant men confronting the Sheriff out on the road. She asked, "Why did they want to do something like that?"

"Well, Loretta, they have a four-fold problem all rolled into one." Doc Ramsey was at his best when he explained things like this.

"I don't mean this to sound confusing, but first, they don't understand. They don't seem to consider this is real life for all of us. Real life has some mysteries, some pain, some unsolved problems, some unanswered questions.

"Second, they don't understand that they don't understand. These are the people who seem to go through life trying to make a square peg fit into a round hole, to use a simple illustration. It never fits but they never stop trying to make it fit.

"Third, they don't want to understand. They deliberately refuse to believe truth even when it should be impossible for them not to see it. Truth is unacceptable to them, it annoys them because it interferes with the way they think and want to live.

"Fourth, they reject truth because, if they accept it, it brings something they fear most of all. It brings responsibility. For some strange reason, they dread to be held accountable for their actions.

"In a nutshell, they don't understand that they don't understand because they don't *want* to understand and be responsible to admit the truth that does not fit their imagined world."

The whole group was amazed at Doc Ramsey's wisdom and impressed with his ability to express it.

Chapter 14

HOW TO CATCH A GHOST

Gerald Jones drove up in his dad's new car. They were rich by most standards of the local people. He went into the shop and found Hob.

"Mr. Herrington, dad wants you to look at this car. It's new, but it's not running good. Sometimes it won't start and it spits and sputters a lot.

Hob said, "Sure, Danny will look at it. We can't do it today, maybe finish by tomorrow afternoon."

When Hob mentioned Danny, Gerald started to say something, but he just turned and left.

When Danny finally got to it he opened the trunk. It was standard procedure in the shop to check the spare tire. It was part of Hob's *Complete Service*.

Looking in, he saw something. "Hmmm, I wonder what this is. A sheet with two holes in it, and a cheerleader megaphone. And what do we have here? A coil of barbed wire nailed to the end of a hoe handle." He inspected it closely. "This looks like ghost equipment."

Gerald was still the school bully and Dill Northcutt was his best friend. Jerry, as they called Gerald, for short, had fought to keep Danny off the football team. But, with Danny's world record field goals in every Middle School game, Jerry was no longer the star, even though he was on the high school team.

What Danny had discovered in Mr. Jones' car gave him an idea. He remembered how scared little Billy Allman had been of ghosts. So one afternoon he took a break and went looking for some equipment he needed for his *plan.* He figured he could find it at the Anderson farm.

He knocked on the door. "Hello Mr.

Anderson, is Doug home?"

"He's in the barn finishing chores."

"Thanks." Danny headed to the barn and found Doug, who was surprised to see him.

"Danny, what brings you here today, town life too dull?"

Danny pointed. "Do you have any extra rope the size you have in the loft pulley, the one you lift hay with?"

Doug nodded. "Sure, what do you need it for?'

"I need it to catch a ghost, and I want you to help me."

Doug walked toward a coil of rope hanging on a hook.. "Will six feet be enough?"

Danny said, "Yeah, that will make a perfect rattlesnake. You still have those rattlesnake rattlers?"

His friend smiled. "Is that part of your ghost catching stuff?" He paused for a moment. "Just what are you up to Danny Herrington? Catching ghosts? Who ever heard of that?"

Danny explained about the Allman's visits from ghosts. He said he knew now that it was Gerald who was scaring little Billy. Danny said, "Do you remember when Gerald was in his Freshman Biology class and one of the guys accidently knocked over the glass case of snakes?"

Doug laughed. "Yeah I remember that. It was all over school how Gerald reacted."

Danny smiled. "The way he got scared and acted like a girl when Bobby Thompson threw that snake on him is still talked about. I heard he even wet his pants. The way I figure it, I can use his fear of snakes against him."

Doug nodded. "Great idea!"

After he completed his plan, Danny visited the Allman's home. Billy remembered him. Ethel asked him to stay for supper. He had planned to stay if they invited him.

He almost ate his weight in pork

chops, mashed potatoes, gravy and corn on the cob. For desert there was hot buttered biscuits with warm sorghum molasses poured over them.

Billy's dad was talking during supper. "Danny, we ain't had book learning and we don't read and write like other people, but we know you are a good man. We heared about Claire and all the meanness she done. We know they took her away but the ghosts said Claire would come get Billy too."

Danny was glad to be here. "Do the ghosts always come about the same time of night?"

"Yes sir."

"Do they always come to the same side of the house?"

"Yes sir. Come take a look"

They went outside. Danny was thinking out loud. "Humm." He saw the large foot prints and the scratch marks on the side of the house. He made some mental notes. He promised Tom and Ethel that he would come back and help

141

them get rid of the ghosts. Finally, before leaving, he thanked them for the supper and gave Billy a hug.

The next day he was talking to Hob at the shop. "These poor people have been beaten down with fear and superstition as though it was a hammer. I can now see the far reaching effect of Claire Rogers' influence more than ever." He paused for a moment. "Dad, I'm having a hard time not wanting to hurt Claire. The more I'm around people with special children, the more I see what she did"

Hob put his hand on Danny's shoulder. "I have that problem too. I cannot remember ever really hating someone, until that day when I heard Dolly explain what they did to her in the home.

"But, we will have people around like Claire from now on. Of course, she's still in jail, but hurting people like her would do no good. She is the kind of person who will never respond to reason. If you were to hurt her, you would really just hurt yourself.

"It is like running over a skunk with your car. All you accomplish is, you smell bad, and there will be another skunk in the road tomorrow. We never run out of them.

"She will eventually poison herself mentally. The poison she has already spread has led to her own undoing. Tyrants are miserable, wretched human beings. Hitler controlled a major part of Europe for a while, but when his power was gone, he killed himself. He just could not face reality."

Danny was beaming at Hob. "Dad you sound a lot like Dr. Ramsey."

The time finally came for Danny to enact his *Ghost Catching Plan.* He met Doug out at their farm so they could work in the barn.

First, he cut off five feet of rope, put the rattle snake rattlers on one end and a three pronged fish hook on the other. He filed the barbs off the hook so it would not stay in if someone was stuck by it. He covered it with a light coat of grease and put a loop in the middle large enough to go over someone's head.

"Doug we need to be there about 9 o'clock tonight. The Allmans know we are coming. They will know we are not the ghosts."

They finished the preparations and drove to the Allman farm. Danny parked about one hundred yards south of the house. He had discovered that the *ghosts* always parked not far away on the north side behind their smoke house.

Danny raised the hood and laid a burlap bag with the rope snake in it on the motor.

He smiled at Doug. "Snakes have to be kept warm at night you know." He thought for a moment. "Okay, I will be at the back of the house, you wait behind the bush and shake it when you hear the rattlesnake rattlers. Then you make a sound like a pig squealing and a hoot owl."

Doug had to practice it a few times.

Danny heard the sound of an engine in the distance. "Here came the ghosts, right on time."

Jerry and his *ghost* friend had grown bolder and confident enough to do without the white sheets ghost usually wear.

Danny waited behind the house with the *snake* in his hands. Doug waited behind the thick bush. Danny shook the rattlers. Doug shook the bush and squealed and hooted. Jerry froze in his tracks. He moved his foot slowly as if to walk back. He heard rattlers behind him.

Danny had sneaked up and dropped the loop over Jerry's head. It was a circus from there on.

Gerald Jones was not known to have a high voice, it was said he was heard at least half a mile away, screaming, "The ghosts have me! Help...help me! Snake...snake!"

His panic stricken sound echoed through the trees as he ran to his car. Dill Northcutt was already in the car with the motor running..

The more he tried to get the snake off his neck the tighter the loop became. He pulled on it only to have one hand slide down to the rattlers and the other hand down to the snake's head. He ran off without his megaphone to make ghost sounds and the wire to scratch on the house.

Ethel and Tom heard the noise and came outside with Billy.

"Danny, I know them ain't ghosts, I know the one who was screaming about the snake, that's the Jones' boy from the hardware store. Have they been donin the ghost things to us all along?"

Danny smiled. "I'm not sure of that, but they are the only ones I know about."

The news spread about the *ghosts* and the circus continued at school. Some of the boys saw the marks all over Jerry. One said, "Man, what happened to you. You look like you have been wrestling with a barbed wire fence."

Dill and Jerry had concocted a story. "Me and Dill was out hunting last night and I got snake bit."

Everybody knew rattlesnakes don't have three fangs, and Jerry had never been hunting in his life.

"A snake with three fangs is a freak, wouldn't you say Danny?" Coach was having fun with this too.

After school, at the hardware store old man Jones was his usual grumpy self. He looked outside.

"Here come those *retarded* people. I'd know those mules anywhere. Son, you take care of them, I have to finish things in the office."

147

Ethel almost ran into the store. She got up in Gerald's face and got right to the point. "You're the ghost and I ain't a standin fer what you're a-doin any more. You hurt Billy with that rock through our winder and I'm here to tell you, we ain't standin fer it anymore."

Poor Jerry; his ignorance and arrogance equaled Claire's. He yelled at her. "Get out of this store you stupid, ignorant, *retarded* women, or I will throw you and your stupid husband and kid out right now."

Faster than the eye could follow, Ethel took a heavy cast iron skillet off the display counter and whacked him in the face, on the neck, in the ribs, on the left knee cap and almost pulverized his left foot before Tom could stop her.

At the same time she was reliving all the times he had scared them, hurt Billy, had torn up their garden. He had damaged their syrup mill, and made them afraid to bring Billy outside in the sun. Her voice echoed in the hardware store and carried down the street to the Sheriff's office.

A passerby saw the mayhem and ran down to his office. "Sheriff, you better come quick, Ethel Allman is in the hardware store, killing Jerry Jones with an iron skillet. He may be dead by now. Hurry!"

The Sheriff jumped up. "What? Ethel Allman? I find that hard to believe."

A minute later he ran into the hardware store. He could not believe his eyes. The six foot two inch Jones lay on the floor, blooded and unconscious. A tiny woman in a homemade flour sack dress, being restrained by her husband, stood over him finishing her angry speech."

The Sheriff eased up to her. "Ethel, I think you need to stop now. He won't hurt you anymore."

Ethel looked up. "Sheriff, are you gonna arrest me?"

"No Ethel, I just need you to put that skillet down and go out to the wagon with Tom and Billy."

A crowd had gathered, filling the store and the sidewalk outside. From somewhere in the crowd a voice quietly said, "Not bad for an uneducated country girl in a flower sack dress, not bad at all. She does not need to be arrested, she needs to be applauded."

And, that's exactly what the crowd did.

The word spread and got around to the auto shop. Hob was stunned. "I still can't believe Ethel Allman did something like that to the Jones's boy. She is one of the most timid people I have ever known. He was a big tough kid. He never lost a fight that I know of. Nobody messed with him."

Lyle said, "Well, you know what they say, LEAVE BABY BEAR ALONE BECAUSE YOU DON'T WANT TO MAKE MAMA BEAR MAD AT YOU."

"Jones," was what Basil Henderson,

his brother-in-law called him when he was angry with him. "You are in a lot of trouble whether you know it or not. What your boy Jerry did to the Allman's baby boy has this whole town ready to hang him, and you too."

"I know," he sighed, "I knew he was playing the ghost and scaring people, but it never was a problem until, well, until that Herrington kid started his freak awareness program."

"LISTEN TO ME!" Basil had had it with his hardware store brother-in-law. "Don't let anyone ever hear you call any of those different children *freaks* again. If your boy is hurt as bad as it looks to me, he may be a freak too. She put some serious hits on his head.

"If you want to save your business, you need to get busy and fix up all the damage Jerry did that can be repaired. You cannot unhurt the Allman baby, but if I were you, I would go see the Allman's and take some lumber and paint and some tools and get busy fixing

151

their house, their fence, their smoke house and especially their syrup mill.

"They made a lot of their living with that mill. I would replace all the meat they lost in their smoke house, I would pay for the money they lost from syrup sales that they did not make. And that would be just to start with.

"If you want to save your hardware business you won't waste any time. A good, sincere, honest, public apology would be a good place to start. It's called confessing you sins. I would send Jerry to visit some relatives a long way from here for about a year.

"And, by the way, his football scholarship just disappeared into thin air. If you have at least two brain cells working you will think about this."

Old man Jones was dejected but his desire for money was more than his loathing of the disabled. He followed Basil's advice.

Chapter 15

97 MILES PER HOUR

Danny worked on the ME 262 German jet engine from time to time. He had made it start a few times, but it just sputtered and flamed out. He pulled on the start engine pull rope until the recoil spring would not return the rope. The engine stayed mounted on the back of the tow truck, on the driver side.

The moonshine men raced their cars weekends when the weather was good. They made a sort of race track in the horse shoe loop of gun barrel road. Nobody knew why, but the road curved around a low place about five or six hundred yards down the road and then straightened out for about three miles.

Hob was stunned when Claire walked into the shop. He didn't realize her lawyer had gotten her out of jail on bail. There had been a long scheduling delay in the trial in Atlanta and the judge had been forced to grand bail to the whole group until they got the scheduling problem fixed. While Hob's mouth was still open she spoke, as if nothing had happened.

"Hob, I'm moving out to the lodge next week. I need my car fixed, it won't start. I need you to come to the house"

It was no surprise when Hob got there and looked under the hood. The distributor was missing.

"Claire, it needs a part I will have to special order. It will take about three weeks."

"I can't wait. Can you get someone to give me a ride?"

Rather than leave her precious Cadillac convertible she asked him to tow it and come out to the lodge and fix it later.

"I can pay you for the tow."

"No need to do that," He said, "you

can pay me when I get the car running."
He went to the shop and sent Danny to
do the job.

Danny came with the big wrecker
truck and started to hook up the car.

Claire frowned. "I thought Hob was
coming."

Remembering Clair's prejudice
Danny was business only; no small talk.
"Dad asked me; he had to take care of
some things out of town."

Claire still would not surrender one
inch of her prejudice, even though she
was pending trial for it. She smirked. "I
will not ride in the truck with a freak!"

Danny just gritted his teeth and
tried to tell her it was not safe to ride in
the car when it was being towed. But
she sat firmly in the seat behind the
steering wheel and refused to move.

Danny did not want her harmed, he
wanted to see her stand trial, but he
would not forgo this opportunity to get
her out of town.

The suspension on the big truck was stiff. It bounced on the road and shook Claire around. She held firmly to the steering wheel and endlessly uttered something in German.

If Divine Providence has a sense of humor it was about to give Claire the ride of her life.

Danny was about a mile from the loop in Gun Barrel Road where the moonshine cars were racing when the jet engine pull rope dangled loose and got caught between the duel wheels of the truck. Danny had mounted the can of diesel to the back bumper of the truck but he had forgotten to take the fuel line out of the can, the last time he tried to start it. With the sudden jerk of the rope the jet engine roared to life.

Danny felt the sudden forward surge of the truck. He heard the roar and knew what had happened. He fought to keep the truck in the road. He could not steer much except straight ahead. The moonshine boys had made banked turns in the loop to allow fast turns.

The big tow truck jumped over the embankment and roared down the track scattering the moonshine cars like frightened sparrows.

J.R. did not look up when he timed the cars, he shouted. "Ninety Seven miles per hours! That's a record!"

Danny held on when he jumped the embankment at the other end of the track. The jet blast burned off the convertible top in minutes. Claire moved to the passenger side and held on.

The huge truck shook the convertible like a rag doll. Danny turned off the truck engine and tried to use lower gears to help brake to a slower speed. This made it possible for him to stay on the road when there were curves.

The last curve before the main road

was at the Mitchell's farm. This would be the hardest one. Bob Mitchell raised cows, hogs, and just anything to make a living. His hog pen was on the outside part of the curve.

Danny tried to make the curve but the car swung up off the ground like a huge wrecking ball. It took off the end of a chicken house and knocked over the outhouse before it slammed against the big oak tree near the hog pen. The tow cable broke with the sudden stop, which catapulted Claire into the hog pen.

Danny managed to get the truck stopped when the jet engine ran out of fuel. He was about a half mile from the wrecked convertible.

Claire was enraged and humiliated to say the least. Danny made it back in the truck in time to see Claire climbing over the fence. She was missing her right shoe.

"I'll get your shoe," Danny volunteered. In spite of all she had done, he was still a gentleman.

He retrieved the shoe from the muddy hog pen. To his surprise a block of wood fell out. It was covered with cloth. It was about two inches high.

Claire could not wear it, so she pulled off her other shoe and took house slippers out of her burned suit case. She walked with a limp to get into the truck.

Her right leg was two inches shorter than her left leg.

When Danny revealed her secret back in town the word spread fast.

"So that was her secret!" Dr. Ramsey mused. "She was desperate to hide it. In her twisted way of thinking, her upbringing forbade admitting it.

Somebody else said, "She lost it in the hog pen? Well that is where she should feel at home."

Claire was never seen in town again. She remained at the Lodge until she was escorted by the Sheriff, back to

Atlanta for her trial.

Chapter 16

MAY CHIN GACE

City Church celebrated their anniversary the first Sunday in September. It was founded in the late seventeen hundreds and was considered a part of the history of the country. Many former members came to town for the occasion and sometimes members of the local government attended.

There was a picnic type gathering Saturday before the Sunday of the anniversary. People brought food, played games, and generally fellowshipped before the winter months would keep most people inside.

However, this year there was an added part to the anniversary. People brought their special children. It was almost strange to see people enthusiastically respond to these children.

People were hugging kids they had

not seen before. Little children were treated to kindnesses withheld in the past by superstition and fear.

Hob stood next to Dr. Ramsey as they silently surveyed the scene. "Hob, I never dreamed one little boy with a big foot and a big heart could bring about a scene such as this. I feel better about our future."

Hob grinned. "You want to know something? My left ear is slightly lower than my right one. I never thought about it until all this started."

Dr. Ramsey mused to himself. *"I wonder how many secret 'freaks' there are among us. It would interesting sometime to find out."*

The next day the church was packed for the anniversary service. The Pastor stood. "My sermon on this Anniversary Sunday is *Allow the Little Children to Come to Me*." He smiled at the full pews. "We will all stand and sing that great hymn Amazing Grace. For our guests who may not be familiar with this hymn, the first line is:

Amazing grace how sweet the sound that saved a wretch like me."

The wood floors, walls and ceiling echoed with the sound of the organ and the voices. With the hymn ended Pastor Richards prepared to begin his sermon when he heard a small voice that was not finished singing. It was Dolly.

"May chin gace, cheat duh choun, chaved uh wetch wak meeeeeeeeeeeeeeeee."

After a short silence he said, "I don't think the angels in heaven can beat that."

The congregation applauded in agreement.

Many of the special children had never been in church before that day. The stigma of it had been broken.

"Pastor, before you begin I wonder

if I may say a word?"

The Pastor nodded to Henry Bennet.

Henry was nervous. "I don't want to seem rude and disrespectful of this church service, but I have to say this. It has been tearing me apart inside and I can't remain silent.

"I'm Henry Bennet. I'm Dolly's father. The parents of the three other children who were mistreated at the home are here. Carl Moore is Bobby's father, Abe Peterson is Sarah's father, and John Phillips is Susan's father.

"We owe a debt of gratitude to Danny Herrington. More than any other person he is responsible for opening our eyes to see the light about our children.

"Claire Rogers, Von Bruner, or whatever her real name is, was able to do what she did because I did not really see my daughter as a person. I was like all the other people who sort of avoided our own kids, like maybe they were not really as human as us. I'm not sure I can

say this as clearly as I now see it.
Ignorance and superstition made us
treat our children, who are different, as
though they were not quite human
enough to have a part in our lives. They
were with us but not fully among us.

"I'm not sure just what to do from
here, but there must be a way to help
our different children get out of the
back bedrooms and into the living
rooms and the front porches.

"Dolly will not ever be able to do a
lot of things, but she can love you
enough to make you feel ashamed. I call
them different children because I can't
think of a better word. I don't think they
were born like this because God is mad
at us or punishing us for our sins.

"I don't have an answer for a lot of
questions that come to my own mind,
but I feel good in my heart that I now
see the light. One more thing; nobody
like Claire or anybody else will ever be
able to put that light out.

"I solemnly swear by the God, of all

that is decent and good, to keep my word. May I die if I do not.

"I never dreamed a man like Gus existed. I have never seriously hurt anyone in my entire life but I did not like to think of what I would do to him if I could. There is no human punishment sufficient to repay him for the damage he has done to my little girl. He does not deserve to be called human. Decent men don't hurt little girls."

There was silence in the church as all eyes went back to the Pastor. Before he could respond another man stood.

"Pastor, since this service has been interrupted may I say a word?"

Again the Pastor agreed.

The man began. "For those who may not know me I'm John Phillips, Susan's father. I think it would be fitting if there could be some kind of an honor or award for Danny Herrington. He is the most responsible for the new light we now see. I have to admit I am ashamed that it took a little boy with a big foot and a big heart to do what we should have done a long time ago. I do not know what anyone thinks about this, but it would be good if there were some good qualified people to teach our different children and maybe work with them.

"Consider this; it is amazing what progress Dolly has made in the short time Danny has worked with her. He has had no formal training but look at what has been accomplished! She can talk, she can walk, she can dress herself. I would be willing to give whatever I can to establish a special school.

"One more thing; Dessie has worked tirelessly day and night to help all of us with special children through this ordeal, and she has not asked for one penny. She delivered my children and I know what I paid her was not really what she deserved. I know her baby boy is deaf and Dr. Ramsey told me he could hear with hearing aids. I don't know what hearing aids cost, but here is twenty dollars to start with to get them." John stood there awkwardly for a moment and then sat down.

Pastor Richards slowly stood and cleared his throat. "Uh…I can't preach a better sermon than those two men just did. This concludes our service. Let us pray."

Those two *sermons* and the events that led up to that day started a new awareness of the needs of special children and a new sense of freedom from the ignorance and embarrassment that the superstition had imposed on people.

The atmosphere in the whole town, to put it simply, seemed to say, *"We are not embarrassed about our different children anymore."*

The money given by John Phillips

and a few others was given to Dr. Ramsey for hearing aids. The doctor wanted Danny to be there when the hearing aids were given to Dessie's son J.J.

Danny watched Dr. Ramsey put the hearing aids in his ears. J.J. reacted with surprise. He reached for Danny. Danny put J.J.'s hand to his throat and said "Jaaaa Jaaaaa. Your name is J.J. Jah, Jah, Jah,"

J.J. tried harder. "Jee, Jee."

Danny held J.J.'s left hand to his throat and his right hand to his own throat. "J.J.,... J.J."

J.J. said more clearly, Jahee, Jahee."

Danny pointed to Dessie and said, "Mama, mama"

J.J. was now smiling ear to ear. He repeated, "Mahee, mahee."

Dessie burst into tears. "My baby can hear, my baby can hear!"

The success of the new hearing aids had been a miracle. Dessie sat on her front porch late into the night with J.J. on her lap. He was mesmerized by each and every sound he heard. Down in the valley a hoot owl nested in a hollow oak tree. Night sounds carry a long distance in the quiet evening. The owl called out and J.J. answered, "Hooooo, hoooooo."

Chapter 17

DINNER WITH THE GOVERNOR

Loretta opened the letter as she walked back from the mailbox. "Danny, this is an official looking letter. I don't think it means you are in trouble, but nobody around here has ever gotten a personal letter from the Governor."

Danny looked up. "What does it say?"

"You can read it yourself"

He looked carefully at the letter. He rubbed his fingers over the bold, black, raised letters. "From the Office of the Governor. It is addressed to Mr. James Daniel Herrington. That's me!"

Hob smiled. "Well, read it to us!"

"It says I am invited to be the guest of honor at a special dinner at the lodge dining room to honor people who have made a contribution to the mental health of our citizens in this state.

"It also says I am to bring my parents and at least two children whom I have helped and their parents also."

"Well, who do you intend to take to this special dinner?"

"I think Dolly and the Bennets, and Billy and the Allmans."

Hob said, "Son, do you think the Allmans will go to this? They might feel very uncomfortable in a formal situation."

I think they'll go if I'm the one who asks them."

Loretta smiled. "Now, how should a man dress to have dinner with the Governor?" Loretta knew neither she, Hob, nor Danny had formal attire for such an occasion."

Danny received a second formal letter that stated the dress for the occasion would be bib overalls, blue jeans, flannel shirts, or the usual work day clothes.

"He really does mean to let everyone know he understands we are just common people and he wants us to know he intends to do something meaningful, not just the usual political talk." Loretta felt her fear about formal attire subside.

Ivory Jones, the main cook at the lodge received the following note from the governor's aid regarding the menu.

"For the Governor's dinner, please serve cornbread, mashed potatoes and gravy, chicken fried steak, green beans, corn on the cob, homemade biscuits, good local homemade jelly, coffee and iced tea. For desert; ask Dessie Thompson to make apple pies and Ethel Allman for advice on other deserts. If you have any questions contact Loretta Herrington."

In preparation for the banquet the Governor came early to meet Danny. In order to make the parents of the special children feel at ease he dispensed with the usual formalities of such a meeting. In order to do that he wore bib overalls and excused his chauffer for the day. All of his staff wore just common looking clothes, some of them, for the first time in their life.

The first thing the Governor asked Danny was about the families he had invited to attend, because he wanted to visit with them before the banquet.

He would get a chance to talk with the Bennets at the lodge but he wanted to meet the Allmans because of the special situation Danny had described.

So, Danny got in the Governor's car and directed him to the Allman's home.

"Tom, this looks like somebody important pullin up in the yard in a new car. Ye better come look."

The Governor got out and stepped upon the porch and smilingly extended his hand to Tom. "Mr. Allman, I'm the Governor, but the most important thing is that I am Joey Rudder's Grandfather."

Ethel asked, "Are you here about the bad men who were playing ghosts and hurt Billy? I really didn't mean to hurt that Jones boy all that bad, but when I found out he was the one that hurt Billy I jist kinda got carried away. He ain't dead is he?

The Governor smiled and said to himself, *"As they say, you hurt Baby Bear, Mama Bear will get you."*

"Ethel, you really didn't do anything wrong. You just did what his parents should have done a long time ago."

The Governor looked at their humble surroundings, with their simple clothes, their mules and wagon and had to pause before he could speak. He was looking at his own childhood.

Finally he said, "Tom, I would like to ask your permission to escort your family to the dinner in your wagon. It's been a long time since I have driven a team of mules but I think I can still do it.

As he drove away from the house with the Allmans in their wagon the Governor smiled to himself as he thought, *"I can't wait to see how Valet Parking will handle this. I feel sure they have never parked a team of mules."*

The dinner was delicious and some people were going back the second, third and fourth time for Dessie's and Ethel's deserts.

Finally, Hob stood and spoke. "Ladies and gentlemen, our community has been through a lot over the last few years. First the war and the loss of so many young men who didn't come home. But recently we have been dealing with another kind of war; a war of ignorance on those with disabilities. Some war veterans have experienced discrimination but the worst discrimination of all has been against those young ones born with imperfections.

"But now, thanks to the finest young man ever born, we have all been shown the light. The Governor of our state has come here today to help spread that light across the entire state. So, I am proud to introduce the Governor of our great state, Governor Lawrence Hughes Baxter."

To resounding applause the governor rose to speak.

"I am just like all of you who have had dreams and wishes you have given up for dead because you saw no hope or help to realize them. They got lost somewhere in your past. You made some attempts but the failures overwhelmed you so you gave them up.

"I had given up ever seeing my grandson Joey do anything but exist as a deformed child. But, when Joe and Barbara told me about Danny Herrington's work, I had to see this for myself.

"I did not know anyone in this state was doing any real work to better the lives and living conditions of our special children until I heard about him. It was by chance that Hob came to get the junk stuff at Joe Rudder's place and Danny met my grandson Joey. I cannot begin to tell you the difference in Joey and Barbara and Joe since Danny's visit. Joey is talking more each day and it won't long until he will walk. He is trying now.

"Also, I know there have been some who have opposed this kind of work. Most of the opposition is simply fear of something as new as accepting our special children into our public lives. However, those who want to actively oppose this are not going to succeed.

"I know about Claire Rogers. This is not her first attempt to suppress an effort to get help for handicapped children. I have here in my hand, which you may see for yourself later, a copy of a Chicago newspaper detailing the Nazi efforts in America to make Hitler's ideas seem good and useful to help make this a better country. The picture on the front page is a bit blurred but the faces are clear enough to tell who they are."

"I will not say more about that, but if my grandson were ever harmed by such as the ones I have heard about, I would bring the hanging rope myself"

He paused and motioned for Danny to join him on the stage.

"For those of you who may not know this amazing young man, this is Danny Herrington. He is almost single handedly responsible for the refreshingly new attitude about our special children."

He turned to Danny. "Danny this plaque is to honor you and your work with our little, handicapped, citizens. The state Health Director will be contacting you for more information and your methods and ideas will be put to use as soon as some organized plans can be made."

The audience erupted into a spontaneous five minute standing ovation.

Danny stood on the stage, quietly embarrassed and accepted the award.

In the foyer, after the ceremony a young man approached Hob and Loretta with a newspaper in his hand.

"Mr. and Mrs. Herrington? I'm Jonathan Wilson, the Governor's personal aide. He wanted me to give you this Chicago newspaper."

Hob held it up and they both looked at it.

"THAT'S CLAIR AND GUS! I know now why she did what she did." Loretta's anger showed.

Danny said, "Dad, it's a good thing mom did not know this until now. She might be in jail herself."

The next day Hob asked Danny to go out to the old house where Claire's children's home was, to get some ideas on how to set it up for a good children's home. Hob told him that the rooms would probably need to be remodeled and the lighting would need to be improved.

As Danny drove toward the old house he looked at the plaque laying on his car seat and said to himself, *"I can't believe all this has happened to me."*

As he came around the curve to face the house. He stopped and couldn't believe his eyes. There was a banner across the front of the building that read:

DANNY HERRINGTON HOME FOR SPECIAL CHILDREN.

A crowd was waiting on the porch.

Dessie came out to greet Danny. He was speechless.

Ethel Allman held Billy, who squealed with delight when he saw Danny. Dolly walked out in front of the crowd and handed him the official key to the front door, and kissed him on the check.

As Danny walked up the steps onto the porch the Governor stepped out of the front door, holding Joey in his arms. He smiled at Danny and said, "Danny, this young man is the apple of my eye; I know you will take good care of him."

The congratulations and celebration continued for more than an hour.

As Danny stepped out of the crowd for a moment a man with a camera approached him. "Excuse me young man, are you Danny Herrington?"

"Yes sir."

"I'm from the newspaper. Can you talk with me a few minutes?"

THE END

Epilogue

I am the little deformed boy. People pass by and look at me, shake their heads and go on. I am the *special* little girl who struggles to understand the big frightful world I look out and see. I am the helpless child with no voice and no one to speak for me. I am kept out of sight.

I hear the voices of my family in the other room living life and enjoying each other. I would like to join them, but they don't come and get me. I am the girl with limited understanding but I have a heart and feelings. When I am abused I cry but no one hears, or cares.

That is the way it was until Danny came. He showed other people it is ok to hug me. I like to be touched and I want to touch you. If you hug me and kiss me it will not make you a freak. If I touch you it will not hurt you, it will not make you a freak. I can't perform great feats like the heroes do, but I can love you more deeply because I know what it is to go without love. I can't write great poetry or music or invent things, but I have music in my heart, which if you could hear it, you would want to sing with me.

I do not know why I was born like I am. I have to live the way I am. I would give the world to be normal like you, but that will never happen. But, I can give my heart to you more completely and with more passion than a *normal* person.

Inside of me is my inmost self. In here, I am an orphan unless someone like Danny comes. He understands and loves me.

If you will be Danny for me, I pom-miss to give you all my heart. I will never turn away from you, I will never betray you. I will be your best friend. I pom-miss.

You can be like Danny if you will.

Do you pom-miss?

ABOUT THE AUTHOR

John Holt grew up a county boy, the sixth child of ten. His family attended a small Baptist Church that needed a congregational song leader when John was fourteen. This was the start of his involvement in music that was to last more than fifty five years.

John, and his wife Lon Nell, are graduates of Arlington Baptist College where he studied music and was the featured soloist in Handel's Messiah, the Opera Il Trovatore and other major productions.

He lives near Columbus, Ohio with his wife, Lon Nell. They have been married fifty three years, have three children, twelve grandchildren, and ten great grand children.

John is still busy in music, is an experienced bee keeper, and a craftsman building special desks and book cases for his special needs grandson Toby, who is the inspiration for this book.

Made in the USA
Middletown, DE
19 February 2016